A DEAL
WITH THE DEVIL

A Novel by

Nicola Jane

To submit a manuscript for our review, email us at

submissions@majorkeypublishing.com

CHAPTER ONE

Bella

I close my eyes and put my head back letting the rain splash against my face. It's been weeks since we've had a good down pour and it feels good against my clammy skin. I press the volume button on my headphones, blasting Drake into my ears.

I can't wait to get in and shower. As much as I love my job, I hate being covered in sticky cake mix and icing sugar.

As I approach the small, semi-detached house, which I share with my dad, I notice the black truck parked outside. It looks out of place in our run-down area, but it must be a visitor for the neighbor. The new girl that has moved in next door seems to have a lot of male callers and most look loaded, not that I'm judging.

I open the front door and fight with my bag. Why can't I just stick my hand in and find my phone? It's literally like Narnia in there; wrappers, deodorant, pens, my kindle. I just want to turn the music off.

I come to an abrupt stop. Standing in front of me is

the biggest guy I have ever seen. For a second, I wonder if he's a statue because he doesn't move, he doesn't speak, he just stands there looking completely cool, rocking a black suit and shades, blocking my entrance to the kitchen.

"Erm, hey," I smile nervously.

He doesn't speak but gives a slight nod of his head to acknowledge that he's seen me.

"Dad!" I don't take my eyes off Mr. Muscle Mountain.

"He's in the kitchen," he says, which makes me jump. He's got such a deep voice it rumbles through me, making me shiver. He notices my reaction because he sniggers, giving a knowing nod. He isn't bad looking at all, I'm sure he's used to getting that kind of reaction from women.

He moves to one side and points in the direction of the kitchen, like I don't know where the hell my own kitchen is. I slowly edge past him, keeping my eyes on him for any sudden movements. Not that I would do much if he suddenly made a grab for me. My height stands at just five-three and I have a tiny, slim frame. It's nothing compared to his large, well-built, mountain of a body. He clearly works out…a lot.

I open the kitchen door to find Dad sitting at the kitchen table looking glum.

"Dad who the hell is that man mountain?" I ask in a hushed tone, hoping the beastly guy doesn't hear me. "I literally almost screamed the house down. Why is he just standing there not doing anything? It's weird. What's going on?"

I place my bag on the table and look up. My Dad is staring past me so I follow his line of vision and then let out a little yelp when I notice another huge guy. He stood at the far end of the kitchen leaning against the wall, watching me with amusement.

"Oh, dear god," I squeak.

"Bella, this is Aiden Tremos." I don't miss the guilty look that crosses my dad's face.

I glance again at the stranger. He is so completely gorgeous that I daren't look him full in the eye in case I faint or make a complete idiot out of myself. He's big, like the man mountain guarding the hall but taller, with the brightest blue eyes I've ever seen. Tattoos crawl across his arms and up his neck. They leave me wondering if he's completely covered. He's dressed in navy suit trousers with a white shirt. The sleeves are rolled up, giving him a casual, yet dangerous look.

He gives me a cocky grin and folds his arms across his broad chest. "Have you finished?" he asks, humor lacing his words.

I feel my face burn with embarrassment, he caught me ogling. I turn back to Dad, who still isn't meeting my eye.

"Please tell me you don't owe money again Dad?"

He looks at Mr. Tremos who moves towards me. "Maybe you'd like to sit down?" he offers, pulling out a chair.

I take a step back. "No, I want to know what the hell is going on."

He grips the back of the chair and bites his lower lip. "Sit, Isabella."

The way he commands, leaves no room for argument and I find myself lowering into the chair. I don't think I should piss this guy off. He's come with backup and who knows what they are into; drugs, gambling? I've recently read that the numbers are on the rise for human trafficking.

"I own a few nightclubs and bars in the area," he explains, sitting across from me. He looks too big to be at this table, in this kitchen. "Your Dad was in one of the bars last night."

I look over at Dad, I feel disappointment start to creep in.

He's been battling alcohol for as long as I can remember. Mum died ten years ago, but it started way before then. I've spent most of my twenty-three years looking after him, putting him to bed whenever he was too intoxicated, working hard to keep this roof over our heads.

Lately, things had improved. Dad had gotten a job at the local fish market and for the last two months he hadn't drank a drop. I was just starting to relax. Stupid me for thinking we had turned a corner.

"Whatever he's done, I'm sorry, okay?" I say. "He isn't well. If it's money, I can pay you back. I just need time."

He puts his hand up, effectively shutting me up. I bite
my lower lip to stop myself from calling him out on that,
I hate rudeness.

"Your Dad doesn't owe me anything, but he was
spouting some crazy stuff and I'm here because I'm
worried he's put you in danger."

Relief floods me for a second, knowing that I won't
have to pay off another debt. My wage is only just
covering everything as it is. But then the words sink in,
he's put me in danger. I glare at Dad, who makes a grab
for my hand. I pull it away before he gets a chance to beg
my forgiveness.

"What kind of danger?"

"He's offered to sell you Bella." I suck in a breath. Of
all the things I was expecting, that definitely wasn't one
of them. Is my Dad into human trafficking? I'm so
confused.

"He what?" I gasp almost choking on the shock of
what he's telling me.

"Bella, I can explain," rambles Dad, tears forming in

his eyes.

"Then please, start!" I stand up and begin pacing the floor.

"I was stupidly drunk. I don't remember much apart from waking up in Mr. Tremos' office. But I've received texts from some nasty pieces of work telling me I owe them,"

he's rambling in his panic to explain himself. The words are taking a while to penetrate my slow, tired brain today.

I look at Mr. Tremos, who is watching our interaction with interest. I put my head in my hands, the reality of what is happening making me feel nauseous.

"My god Dad, just when I think you can't possibly fuck up anymore," I mutter quietly. "When you say sell, what do you mean exactly? For work?" I ask, looking directly at Mr. Tremos.

He glances at my Dad, then back to me. "No Bella, your virginity."

I freeze, open mouthed, looking from him to my Dad. It's like a story from one of those stupid books I've been reading. I feel my Dad drop to the floor in front of me. Yes, I am a twenty-three-year-old virgin! People tell me it's something I should be proud of, but I'm not. It's like a bad omen, always hanging over me. It brings me stress whenever I meet someone new, becomes some big deal, and then before I know it, everything becomes about that instead of me.

"I don't know what I was thinking Bells, I'm so sorry," says Dad, interrupting my thoughts.

"You need to go Dad, this is the final straw," I whisper, hurt evident in my voice. How could he do this? I'm his daughter. If I'd have spent less time caring for his drunken ass, then maybe I would have had more time to date and meet someone worthy of my virginity.

He looks at me confused. "It's not safe for you to stay here sweetheart, not on your own. What if these guys come looking for you?"

"And where the hell am I supposed to go?"

He rubs my arms, sheer panic on his face. "Go back to Carl, just for a bit?"

I shove him away and he falls back, landing on his

ass.

"Go back to Carl! Are you serious right now? You think I'm safer with that maniac? Have you forgotten what he did to me? I hate him, more than I hate you right now and that's saying something!"

"Bella he's a cop. He will keep you safe, who's going to come after a cop's girl?" he says, trying to convince himself more than me. "Besides, he's expecting you."

I glare at him. "You just went ahead and planned that? You didn't even talk to me about it. First you sell me and then you dump me on the biggest asshole you can find."

"Well when I realized what I'd done Mr. Tremos here suggested I find you somewhere safe to stay. I didn't know where else was safe. I didn't want to put Aria in any danger. I just thought Carl owes you one and he said he'd be happy to help out."

Of course he would. He's been trying to get in my knickers from the second he realized I was still a virgin. Creep.

Mr. Tremos stands, pulling my attention to him. He

makes a show of refolding his shirt sleeves.

"I'm sorry we met like this Bella. Good luck with..." he pauses and then adds, "everything."

I place my hands on my hips. "Really, that's all you've got?"

He stops at the door and turns back to face me. "Sorry?" he asks, confused.

"You come in here with that scary gorilla out there and you get all like, 'Hey Bella your Dad sold your ass to some dodgy bastards,' and then you just get up and go? I thought you were concerned for my safety!"

He gives a laugh. "I really don't sound like that."

"Did you buy me?"

He laughs again and shakes his head. "No, I turned the offer down."

"Why?" I ask, offended. "Am I not good enough?" I can't believe I've just said that, I inwardly cringe, but it's out there now and I'm on a roll. I'm just delaying him leaving. I feel safer with him and his guard dog here.

He begins to walk towards the door. Again, and I feel panic, like if he leaves, something bad will happen.

"What shall I do?" I ask.

He shrugs, pats the man mountain on the back, and they leave. I stand there like a goldfish, my mouth opening and closing.

What the actual fuck just happened? This stuff doesn't happen in real life, in MY life!

CHAPTER TWO

Aiden

I did the right thing, I went and told the girl what her dumbass Dad was doing, but then he mentioned the damn cop and that was my cue to leave.

Fuck! Raff said it would be easy, that she would be putty in my hands, but she really doesn't seem like the putty kind.

Her Dad had told me previously about an ex-boyfriend that she could stay with, one that she had no interest in any longer, but he failed to mention it was the cop, a cop that I know very well. I'm going to kick Raff's dumb ass when I get back to the club. What's the point in having him do background checks and research if he misses huge details like that?

"Thought she was coming with, Boss?" asks JP.

"Yeah me too. Raff's an idiot. She's the ex of Carl, as in Cop Carl!"

"Oh. That's not good then. Do we have a plan B?"

"Who knows what Raff has come up with for plan B? He couldn't even get plan fuckin' A right!"

We arrive at Tremos, one of my nightclubs. I shove open the club door in frustration and it bangs back against the wall, the hinges creaking in protest.

"Raff you dumb fuck! Where the hell are you?"

He appears from behind the bar, topless and pulling up his jeans, a wide grin across his face. I roll my eyes. I'm out pulling in the girl and he's fucking some girl.

"Aid, where's the girl?" he asks, pulling a blond to her feet. She wipes her mouth then totters off towards the bathroom, butt naked. We all watch her tiny ass before I turn back to him.

"Cop Carl's ex missus you mean?" I ask, chucking my suit jacket on the nearest bar stool.

"What? No way, I checked her out man; she's never been with anyone. Jake was very clear about her."

"Then tell me why she's heading there right now!" I grab a glass and pour a shot of whiskey. I knock the amber liquid back, wincing as it burns, and then I slam the glass on the bar.

"I'm running out of time jackass!"

He buckles his belt. "Her hospital records did show an

assault about a month ago, it's how I know she was still a virgin, cos they checked she hadn't been raped. Just cuts, bruises and a broken wrist. You reckon that was Carl's work?"

I shrug my shoulders. "Possibly, she did say he had done something to her."

"Then that's it big man," smiles Raff, slapping my back. "Swoop in there, rescue the chick from the big bad ex, and then she will come running willingly."

I drop my head to the bar and groan. "This is why I don't do this shit. Too much hard work."

Bella

Carl sits back on the sofa, a huge smug grin across his face.

"I told you you'd be back."

"You're a cop; cops protect people and right now I need protecting, but please don't get it twisted Carl, let's call this your apology for landing me in hospital."

"Call it what you want Bella. Go and unpack your shit."

I sit on the edge of the double bed, looking around the room in disgust. It's a typical bachelor pad, black silk sheets on the huge bed but not much in the way of furniture. There's a mirror on the opposite wall to the bed and I can only imagine the reason Carl would have it positioned there.

How the hell did I end up back here? Surely, I'd be just as safe with Aria.

Aria is my best friend. We grew up together. She owns the bakery where I work and lives above it in a cozy little apartment.

She's petite like me, standing at just five-foot-two,

but she's fiery, and I reckon she could keep me safe. I smile at the thought. She's going to screw when she knows I'm staying here with Carl, she hates him.

I met him a few months ago; he was on duty and looked like every girl's dream in his uniform. We got to chatting in Costa and I agreed to go out for a drink with him. He was charming, funny, and the fact he had a great body and a gorgeous face to match helped. We began seeing each other but Carl got fed up of taking things slow. Three months into the relationship we began arguing a lot, so I ended things. He became obsessed with getting me into bed and it was such a turn off.

Last month I bumped into him on a night out, things got ugly fast and he hit me. I ended up in hospital with a broken wrist. Don't get me wrong, I'm no damsel in distress. I didn't sit sobbing while he hit me, I fought him with everything I had which is probably the reason I came off worse. Luckily, some security guys from a nearby club broke it all up.

I didn't press charges. Aria was so mad at me, but I didn't see the point. Carl is a slippery little fucker, he would have gotten off the charges somehow and I didn't want the stress of a court hearing with everything I had going on with Dad. The thought of standing up in court and explaining that he was pissed off because I wouldn't give him my virginity gives me hives. The fact that I'm still a virgin at the ripe old age of twenty-three is embarrassing enough.

I decided cutting contact was the best way. Carl came to see me in hospital and apologized. He loves his job and agreed to stay away from me and up until this point he's stuck to his word.

Aiden

I flick through the pictures of Bella. She really is stunning. Long brown hair going all the way down to her rounded ass, a tiny, slim waist, c-cup perky tits, blue eyes, and a perfect smile with lips begging to be kissed. If I was the kind of person to feel, I'd definitely feel something for this beauty.

I drop the pictures back into the file and pick up the paper work. I stare at my brother's signature at the bottom and shake my head. That son of a bitch must have thought he was so funny drawing up these papers.

I'm interrupted by a knock on the door.

"Enter."

JP appears. "Hey Boss, just thought you would want to know that the girl is waiting to get in."

My head snaps up to him. "What?"

He nods and points to one of the CCTV monitors on the wall opposite me, "See."

Sure enough, Bella is in the line, dressed to impress in a skirt that's barely there with a group of females.

"Go get her in JP and try not to scare the shit out of

her this time."

He nods and disappears.

Bella

"I feel like it's too short Ari." She knows I hate revealing clothes, it makes me uncomfortable to be on show. I tug the bottom of the dress that just about covers my ass.

"Jesus Bells, chill out will yah? It's a night out, you have to dress to impress."

"Impress who? In case you have forgotten, I'm back staying with Carl," I remind her. She rolls her eyes.

"A relationship of convenience doesn't count."

"I feel like Carl won't agree with that statement," I laugh out, but it soon fades when I notice the man mountain from earlier heading towards us. The gorgeous god like man did say he owned a few nightclubs.

He stops in front of me. "Follow me," he orders and turns leading us inside. I look at Aria who shrugs, but then follows him.

He takes us up a flight of stairs and opens a door.

"Tonight, you are all VIP guests to Mr. Tremos."

I stare around the crowded room, full of important looking people.

"Wow," I mutter "Thanks." He nods his head once and then leaves.

Aria gives a little squeal. "Is that the guy?"

"One of them. Mr. Tremos must own this place. I never connected the name," I say, looking around at the huge chandeliers hanging low above the bar. The place is amazing and way better than the main bar downstairs.

Four Porn Star Martinis later and I'm feeling the buzz. The bartender is amazing, not only is he stunning to look at, but he makes the best drinks.

"So, Raff," slurs Aria. "Tell us more about Mr. Tremos."

He grins, "Why don't you go over and ask him what you want to know?"

I freeze and glance over to the spot that he's nodding towards. Aiden is sitting in a booth with two blondes on either side of him, talking to another man in a suit. He suddenly looks at me and I look away, embarrassed he caught me staring.

"Fuck," I mutter.

"Fuck indeed," says Aria with a slight smirk crossing

her face.

"What?" I ask in a panic. I daren't look back in case he catches me again, but curiosity is getting the better of me, and then I feel him. My skin prickles and I know he's there.

"Bella, what are you doing here?" his deep voice makes me shiver. I take a deep breath and then I turn to face him.

"Mr. Tremos, thank you for the VIP treatment."

"Well, as it's not safe for you to be out and about, I thought it better you be where I can keep an eye on you." His voice is stern and suddenly, I feel like I'm a naughty child.

He presses a finger to his ear and then says something into his wrist. I want to laugh at the James Bond style gadgets but the serious look on his face tells me I shouldn't.

"I am quite capable of looking after myself, but thanks again," I say, bringing his attention back to me.

I smile and turn my back on him. He leans in, and when I feel his front press against my back, I stiffen slightly.

"Do not turn your back on me Bella." He uses that growly voice again and I fidget against him. "If you keep pressing your ass against my cock like that, I may just have to take your father up on his offer."

I hold my breath and I hear him laugh as he moves away. No one has ever spoken to me like that and I can't deny that his choice of words sends sparks straight to my core.

"Bella!" My heart drops, it's Carl.

"Oh great," sighs Aria.

Carl grabs my arm and spins me to face him. "What the fuck are you doing in here? I told you to stay at home!" He is in my face. "How can I keep you safe if you're out here while I'm at work?"

I shove him from me, and he stumbles back.

"How did you even get in here?" I rub my arm where he grabbed me, noting there's already a red mark.

"The door staff asked my permission to let him up," smiles Aiden. "I thought he was your boyfriend, aren't you staying with him?"

"Well thanks for your help," I say sarcastically. "No, he's my ex!"

CHAPTER THREE

Aiden

She's pretty. Even when she's mad with her gorgeous, flawless face all screwed up with anger. My god does she smell good, all vanilla and fresh. Being so close to her makes me want to drag her off and lock her away, only letting her out to pleasure me with those plump lips. I watch this creep yelling at her and notice JP glaring at me.

"What?" I mouth shrugging.

He points to Bella, who I note is giving as good as she gets. "Save her," he mouths, and I laugh. I will, just not yet.

Bella's friend nudges her arm against mine.

"Hey, fancy a drink?" she gives me a cute smile. "We could be waiting for this to die down for a while," she says, nodding at Bella and her boyfriend arguing.

I indicate to JP to get us a drink and then I guide her over to my booth.

"Your friend always like this with her fella?" She looks over at them still in a heated discussion.

"Bella hates him; she just needs a place to stay for a whi+le and he isn't her fella, just an ex."

"Can't she stay with you?" I nod a thanks at JP, as he places our drinks down on the table.

"The plan," he whispers in my ear, but I shoo him away, much to his annoyance.

"She doesn't want to bring trouble to my shop," she explains.

This must be Aria, the cake shop owner and Bella's best friend. She's pretty, in an English rose kind of way. Pale skin but rosy cheeks and large brown eyes. Her brown hair is cut short and it suits her small oval face. She's very petite and if I didn't have my sights set on her friend, I'd consider seducing her.

"She must have other friends she can stay with?"

"There's Jack, but he's just moved his boyfriend in, so she doesn't want to put on him. She's spent so much time looking after her Dad that she's kept her circle small."

I watch Carl grab Bella and try to drag her from the club. I guess this is where I swoop in to save the girl. I stand and fasten my suit jacket as I head over to them.

"Let her go," I say it firmly. I hold all the authority in this club, and I don't appreciate this idiot causing a scene in my VIP area where some of the top socialites hang out, including the top dogs that sign his paycheck.

"Who the hell are you to tell me what to do Tremos? This is my girl and I'm taking her home!"

"She doesn't want to go with you, Harris. I suggest you let her go before I call DCI Caine and tell him what a fuss you are causing in my club."

He lets go of her arm and shoves her towards me. I catch her and steady her.

"Keep her, she's too much trouble anyway, and don't get your hopes up, she doesn't put out!" He storms off.

"Are you okay?" I ask, turning to Bella, but she doesn't look happy at all. In fact, she looks like she's about to explode.

"Why do you keep jumping in to defend my honor? I can look after myself!"

I stand there baffled as she storms towards Aria. *Win her over,* they said. *It'll be easy*, they said. I shake my head in confusion.

I catch Raff and JP laughing behind the bar, they must think all this is hilarious. Jake's probably up there with the big man, killing himself laughing. Bastard.

I join the girls, seeing as they are sitting in my private booth.

"So," smiles Aria, staring between me and Bella. "That went well." Bella throws a peanut at Aria's head and she dodges it, laughing.

I wave my hand in Raff's direction indicating that I need more drinks.

"Does everyone just serve you when you wave your hand like that?" asks Aria.

I shrug. "Usually." What's the point in owning a club if you have to serve yourself?

Once the drinks arrive, I settle back in my seat, observing the banter going back and forth between the girls.

Bella

I swallow my drink down in one go because I feel uncomfortable. Carl's completely ruined my night and now I'm stressing about where I'm going to go tonight. If I was a normal girl of my age, I would probably hook up with some random guy and spend the night with him, only I'm not normal. I'm starting to feel like holding onto my virginity for the right one has become a hindrance. It's not like I woke up one day and decided I was going to save myself, it just kind of happened. I haven't met a man that I've wanted to go that far with. The thought brings my attention to the gorgeous god, sitting opposite me.

"Do you own this club?" Aria is quizzing him.

"Sort of." He finishes another drink and indicates to the bar that he needs a refill. It must be nice to hold that much power and boy can he drink a lot.

"How can you sort of own a bar? You either do or you don't. Why did you turn up at Bella's today?"

He shifts in his seat looking uncomfortable. "She already knows why."

"No, I want the real reason," insists Aria. "Why

would some hot, club owning man, with people that run around after him, just turn up and pre-warn a girl about that? Why would it bother you what happens to her?"

I feel like I should jump in and rescue him from her never-ending questions, but I want to know the answer to this one. Aria has got a point.

Suddenly, I'm shoved along the booth by the bartender. He grins at me and I'm squashed up next to Aiden.

"Hey gorgeous ladies, your night doesn't look very fun from where I'm standing."

"We were trying to get to know this mysterious man here, but he's not giving much up," says Aria.

Raff looks at me with a mischievous grin. "You want to get to know my man here Bella?"

I feel myself go red and I stare at my fingers. "It's Aria that wants to know him, not me," I'm mumbling with embarrassment. I kick Aria under the table.

She laughs, "I just find it odd that he keeps popping up to rescue Bella. Are you even single?"

Aiden gives Raff a warning glance, but I catch it and

once he realizes, he stands.

"If Bella wants to ask me shit then she can do it herself, we aren't in high school!"

We watch in surprise as he stomps away. Raff shakes his head like he's disappointed.

"Don't mind him, he gets moody quicker than a woman. No offense."

We carry on our night, shots and various cocktails are constantly being brought to the table, all compliments of Mr. Tremos.

Aiden occasionally reappears, he chats with various people and then disappears again.

I'm starting to feel sick and I realize that I haven't been this drunk in a long time. I don't even know where the other girls went that we arrived with.

I stand and grab onto the table to steady myself.

"Toilet," I say as a way of explanation when Aria and Raff stop their conversation to look at me.

I stumble my way to the toilet and stand in the line. You would think that VIP's didn't have to wait. I pull out my phone and notice I have fifteen missed calls from

Carl.

"Wanker," I mutter deleting the calls.

"Charming," rumbles a deep voice from behind me. I jump, dropping my phone.

"Shit." I bend to get it and lose my balance, falling on my ass. I look up at Aiden, who doesn't look amused by my stumbling, drunken self. He reaches down and pulls me up by my arms.

"Come, you can use my bathroom."

I rub my ass then shove my phone back in my clutch bag. How many times can I possibly embarrass myself in front of him?

Aiden leads me back through the club. His huge hand encasing mine. He stops by the booth and says something to Raff and Aria. They look mighty cozy. Aria giggles and waves at me.

Aiden continues through the club and then enters an office. There's an elevator door just inside and he pushes a button. It arrives, he pulls me inside, and we wait in silence as the lift ascends to the next floor. My mind plays different scenarios on a reel; him kissing me, pushing me against this elevator wall and demanding I fuck him. I press my thighs together, trying to ease the ache that he is unaware he is creating.

The doors open into a lobby. It reminds me of a hotel. There's a large white door directly in front of us. He leads me through a door, and I am stunned by a huge open space with floor to ceiling windows looking out over London.

"Wow, you're like Christian Grey." He rolls his eyes. "But you look like that actor, yah know, the one from Game of Thrones, Drogo." He leads me to the kitchen area and sits me on a stool. "Oh my god, you really do, what's his name?" I say it more to myself than to him.

He sighs and hands me a glass of water. "Jason Momoa."

"Yes, that's him! You look just like him, only without all the hair. I really need to pee."

I stand and wobble, he runs around the table to steady me then leads me to the far end of the room.

He opens another door and we enter a huge bedroom. Again, there are floor to ceiling windows and a French door is open, letting the cool, summer breeze blow the curtains.

"OOO, are you going to seduce me Draco?" I giggle. He shoves me through another door and I'm in a bathroom. The lights flick on and I'm temporarily blinded by the brightness.

"Hilarious," he huffs. "Now pee."

I fumble about lifting my tiny skirt. He turns away and heads back out of the door. Once I've finished, I open his bathroom cabinet. Aria reckons you can tell a lot about a man from what he keeps in here. It's all very neat and tidy, bottles of expensive looking aftershave all lined up. Painkillers, a razor, and a comb. Nothing exciting.

I wander back through to his bedroom. It's clean and bright. Nothing like Carl's. The sheets are white cotton, not a crease in them. I run my hand over them, loving the feel of the cool cotton against my hot skin. The next thing I remember is crawling onto the cool sheets and laying there, relaxing as the breeze blows over my body, from the open French door.

Aiden

"I'm serious JP it's not funny!" I'm whisper yelling into the phone. "She is completely naked and she's on top of my bed. What am I supposed to do?"

I knew I shouldn't have rang him, useless bastard. I left her for two minutes and when I went back, she was laying on top of my bed completely naked, fast asleep.

"Bet she as the most gorgeous pair of tits. Is she tanned everywhere?" he laughs. When I don't respond, he calms himself down. "Okay, just chuck a blanket over her. I'm sure she will be mortified when she wakes up but see this as a way into her life. She will respect that you didn't try anything with her and that you took care of her when she was wasted. Girls love that shit."

I disconnect the call and quietly creep back into where she's curled up on my bed. She is tanned everywhere I note as I pull a blanket from my built-in wardrobe.

I freeze when I hear her moan. "I'm sorry, please don't!"

She's clearly having some kind of nightmare. I feel

like I'm intruding, so I start to back out. She suddenly cries out. I place the blanket over her quickly so that I can make my escape but she grabs my arm. I'm frozen to the spot, staring at her tiny hand gripping my thick, tattooed wrist.

"Stay," she whispers, and I can't tell if she's still dreaming. She gives me a gentle tug. "Please Aiden, stay with me."

She shuffles over and gently tugs me until I lay down. *Well this is an unexpected turn. I didn't even have to make an effort,* I muse.

I lay on my back and hold my breath, she crawls against my side and snuggles down, burying her face into my arm.

"Thank you," she murmurs, and then I hear her light snores. I lay wide awake for some time, trying not to notice the heat of her warm, naked body pressing in to my side.

CHAPTER FOUR

Bella

Oh gosh, my head. I groan before stretching out and then I freeze as memories of last night flood my mind. *Oh god, oh god, oh god!* I squeeze my eyes tight. *Please don't let it be real.* I slowly open one eye and then squeeze it shut again. Yep that confirms it, the memories are real. *Crap, crap, crap!*

A cough makes me jump and my eyes shoot open.

"Morning sunshine." Aiden is smirking, and I want to slap it off his gorgeous face.

"Why am I naked?" My voice is croaky, dry from all the alcohol and I pull the blanket tight around me. He grins wider.

"You called me Khal Drogo."

I throw my forearm over my eyes. "No I didn't."

"Oh, you did. Do you often play out fantasies Bella? Or should I say Daenerys." I can hear his sniggers.

I pull the pillow over my head and hold it there to hide my embarrassed, crimson colored face. I'm sure I would remember saying that, but he does look a bit like him, it was my first thought when I saw him at my Dad's house.

"Your phone's been ringing non-stop, I think Carl's getting annoyed." I peek out from under the pillow and he's holding my phone, flicking through it. "Call me before I track your mobile and come and find you," he reads it with a smugness in his tone. "He really isn't a nice guy, is he? So clingy and desperate."

I sit bolt upright. "Shit, where's my clothes?"

He shrugs his large shoulders. "You took them off."

"Aiden help me. If he comes here, he will go mad. I can't deal with him today, I feel like crap," I say desperately.

He holds out my phone, so I can see it. "Can I post this on your Facebook?" It's a selfie of me and him, I'm clearly passed out and he's grinning up at the camera, doing a thumbs up.

"Delete that right now. Are you trying to ruin my life?"

I climb from the bed, keeping the sheet wrapped around me and I stomp into the bathroom. Once inside, I drop the cover and begin getting dressed.

I go through his drawers until I find some toothpaste alongside several unopened tooth brushes. Clearly, he has a lot of overnight visitors. I'm surprised that the thought bothers me slightly.

Aiden

I click 'add photo' and upload the image of me and Bella to my Facebook. I don't often use it but if I want to get this girl, I need to start stirring up some shit between her and lover boy. *That's the first time I've had a naked girl in my bed that's slept the whole night without putting out*, I muse.

She appears looking disheveled but still beautiful. I mentally slap myself, since when do I see anyone as beautiful? Fuckable yes, but never beautiful.

"I've deleted the pic from your phone, after I sent it to mine."

Her face drops. "Why? Why would you send it to yourself?"

"Memories Bells," I tease. "Not often I role play. Although many girls have compared me to Drogo," I say it proudly.

She huffs and opens her phone. Its buzzing in her hand.

"Hi Carl, so sorry, I passed out at Aria's place," she lies easily but her face shows that she is uncomfortable doing it. I can hear him yelling and she moves the phone from her ear slightly.

"Don't be like that, I'm sorry I worried you. I will make it up to you," she soothes, glancing at me.

I role my eyes and pour a coffee, setting it down in front of her. "Well maybe not that, I thought we agreed you were just helping me out," she whispers her words, trying to prevent me from hearing.

He yells some more. "I'm not teasing you Carl. Look I don't want to talk about this over the phone, I will see you after your shift." She disconnects the call, looking annoyed.

"Lover boy getting fed up of waiting?" I smirk.

She sits opposite me at the large island in the middle of my kitchen area.

"What are you waiting for anyway? If you love him, what's the problem? Or are you waiting for a ring to be put on it?"

She blushes. "No, I just don't feel it with him."

"Feel what? Please don't tell me you're a fairytale kind of girl. If you're waiting to be struck with cupid's arrow, you're going to be very disappointed. All you're going to feel is pain and then relief when it's over."

She glares at me. "I just want to feel comfortable with the person I'm with like that and Carl is not that person."

"Then stop using the guy!"

She looks annoyed again. "My Dad didn't give me much choice!"

I shake my head. "Don't use excuses Bella, your Dad fucked up but surely you have other people you can run to. I feel for this guy, he's holding out for your cherry and you have no intention of giving it to him. No wonder he's frustrated and pissed at the world, holding out can send a guy nuts!"

"Maybe I should just do it then, just to get rid of it. That will solve all my problems, my Dad can't sell what I don't have!"

I feel an anger rise inside me. I grip the table.

"No!" I grit out and she looks at me in surprise.

"You said I was teasing him," she mutters it like a stroppy teenager.

I need to get my shit together. Why am I so mad?

Yes, I need her to be a virgin but I'm going about this all wrong.

"Look not to be rude, but I have stuff to do," I say.

She stands up. "Sorry, and I'm really sorry about making a fool of myself last night."

"JP will drop you off, wherever you need to go. He's waiting in the lobby." She nods and gathers her bag. "And Bella, if you need anything, you know where I am."

Raff appears as she exits, "Tell me you didn't fuck her yet?" I smack him across the head.

"No, I didn't sleep with her, I'm not stupid!"

He helps himself to coffee. "You need to play the long game with this one or you're going to lose the lot!"

"Don't you think I know what's at risk Raff? I just don't know how to do all this, you know what I'm like, I need rules, I need control and knowing that I can't just go in there and claim her is too hard. All this work bores me," I huff, and he laughs.

It's a running joke. I don't settle down, which is why Jake has done what he's done. Me, Jake, JP, and Raff have always been close. Jake, my non-identical twin, died a few months ago, up until that point we were all inseparable, right from school.

We were pranksters, always playing tricks on each other, never taking life too seriously. None of us had really settled down, although at one point or another we have all been in a serious relationship. That is how I know relationships aren't for me.

When I met Laurie, I was just 20, I loved her fiercely, I became possessive and obsessed until I pushed her away. Losing her tore me apart and I refused to put myself or any other girl through that again. I still see her. She's married now and every time she hits a rough patch, she turns to me. It's not healthy, but I can never find it in me to turn her away.

Her husband is a rich prick, he owns a massive hotel chain and most of the time he treats Laurie like shit, but she insists she's happy.

"Did you get anywhere with her friend?" I ask.

"No, I'm a gentleman," he grins. "She wants the chase, I can't be bothered with that shit. I fucked some random out in the alleyway instead!"

"Classy! Aria's nice, if I wasn't chasing Bella, I would definitely have a go at her. But you're right, they both seem to be hard work. Cracking Bella is going to take weeks. No wonder Jake gave me two months."

"Look man, whose to say we haven't planned this all wrong? Go in there as you, stop keeping that beast under lock and key, maybe she would like your dominant, bossy ass to take charge!"

I ponder his suggestion.

Bella

Carl storms across the room and pins me to the wall, I don't even have time to register what's happening before he slaps me hard across the face. Tears rush to my eyes as my vision blurs. He holds his phone next to my face.

"What the fuck is this?" It's the picture that Aiden took.

He grips my neck tightly and I cough, trying to gasp some air into my lungs.

"Carl!" it comes out as a whisper. I can feel my windpipe crushing under his strength.

"Six months Bella and you give it to this bastard!" He shoves me to the floor and lands a punch to my stomach, making me double over.

"I didn't!" a sob leaves my already sore throat, "I didn't! I fell asleep there, that's all!"

"Prove it." His large hands swoop down, gripping my skirt. I try to shove him away, but he pushes it up and over my hips.

"Don't do this Carl, please don't do this!" I'm begging while shuffling backwards, trying desperately to get away.

"You know he's a player, right? A fuck em and chuck em kind of guy. Did you fancy a bit of rough sex, Bella?" He laughs pulling at my knickers. I kick his hand and he slaps me again. I feel warm liquid and realize my nose is bleeding.

He grips my top and pulls it, tearing it in half.

"I want to see what all the fuss is about." He gropes hard at my breasts.

There's a bang and Carl is ripped off me. I scramble back until I hit the wall. It takes me a second to work out that JP is on top of Carl punching him over and over.

"Stop!" I cry, rushing over and pulling at JP's arm. He pauses, his arm in mid-air, and looks at me, rage evident on his face.

"Get your stuff," he orders me. I rush to the bedroom and grab the suitcase I hadn't unpacked yet.

CHAPTER FIVE

Aiden

I squeeze the thighs that are on either side of my legs, enjoying the feel of her ass brushing against my hard cock. The girl is stunning, but I can't get Bella's smile out of my head. Jesus, I need to stop this shit.

I reach around, my hands running across her stomach, working upwards towards her perfect, rounded breasts. She moans, throwing her head back and grinding harder into my lap. I grip her hair and bite her neck, gently nipping at her skin. I close my eyes and picture Bella. The girl is too impatient, her hand is already between her legs, rubbing herself.

The door opens and JP walks in, he glares at me.

"We have company." He looks pissed as hell.

"Good, I love an orgy!" I grin, slapping the girl's ass. She yelps and pushes against me harder. Clearly, she loves it rough.

When I look back towards JP, he moves to one side and Bella appears. She's wrapped in JPs hoody, it's huge on her but man does she look sexy as hell.

It's then that I notice blood on her face. I shove the girl off me and dive up, rushing over to her.

"Shit, what happened?"

She takes a step back, away from me and towards JP.

"He saw your little photo!"

Tears stream down her face and bitterness laces her words. Shit, I didn't think he would turn on her, I just needed him to kick her ass out. I knew he would see it, I have half of the police force on my Facebook. They think they are being clever keeping tabs on me when in fact I let them see what I need them to.

"Jesus Bella, I'm so sorry." I take her hand. "Let's get you cleaned up. JP get rid of her." I nod towards the naked girl sitting on my sofa looking really pissed off.

I sit Bella in the kitchen and pull out a first aid box. I rummage until I find some antiseptic wipes and gently dab her face.

"I can do it," she says, trying to take the wipe. I keep hold of it. I want to take care of her, this surprises me.

"Bella, sit still," I say firmly, and she does.

Bella

I sit quietly while he cleans my face. I press an ice pack to my cheek.

"You're staying here," his voice is back to being bossy, but I can't deny I feel a thrill at his words.

"I can't stay here, I don't even know you!"

He raises an eyebrow. "Bella you're staying here!" Something in his look tells me he usually gets what he wants.

Later, I watch him as he moves around the kitchen making me a sandwich. Apparently, he never does this and usually orders in or gets someone else to make it for him. I smile as he rips the bread with the butter.

"Shall I help you with that?" I ask, taking the knife from him.

"I have to go to one of my other clubs tonight. Why don't you bring Aria and come for a few drinks?"

"I don't think that's a good idea. My face is a mess and besides, I don't want to cramp your style." Inside my heart is screaming that I really do want to cramp his style.

"You look beautiful, even with the cuts, and bruises

and everyone knows I don't settle down, so you really won't cramp my style." My heart twinges a little and I remind myself that he's just being a nice person, he's not offering to marry me.

Aiden

I've been at the club an hour now. I'm constantly staring at the CCTV monitors watching out for Bella. I think I've been possessed. I left ahead of her, women take forever to get ready, I'd forgotten that fact, but she said she wouldn't be long, and it's been an hour already.

"So, what's the plan now?" asks JP, interrupting my thoughts.

"I still need to play it cool. I've got to reel her in, she loves a bastard, so I've got to play the role."

"Play the role? Aiden, you are the biggest bastard I know. Just be yourself."

"I'm pulling the friendship card at the moment, I need to make her want me." I grin up at him. He rolls his eyes in amusement.

"I thought you couldn't be bothered to play games."

I don't ever play games when it comes to women, but this feels like one big game, my brother being the games master.

I finally see her enter the VIP area, she takes my breath away. Her dark hair flows in waves around her shoulders and the short black dress she's wearing shows all her perfect curves.

"Damn she's fine," mutters JP. I glare at him.

He holds his hands up in a defense kind of gesture with a huge grin on his face. "Just being honest man," he laughs.

Later, I sit in the VIP lounge with a girl either side of me. There is never a shortage of willing girls to keep you company when you own a popular nightclub. Bella is at the bar with Aria, doing her best not to look at me.

The girls reach across for each other and begin kissing. I smile as I watch, letting them run their hands along my jean clad thighs. I see Aria nudge Bella and she sneaks a look as one of the girls begins to kiss my neck. I stand and take a hand of each girl, leading them away to my office. Bella follows every step with her eyes. She needs to feel like I'm not after her in that way.

Bella

"Wow Bells, what I wouldn't give to be one of those bitches right now," Aria sighs.

"Eww Ari, please don't lower yourself. Why would you want to sleep with him? Who knows what diseases he carries. He was with a different girl earlier at his house!" I screw my face up to show my disgust.

"When you've lost that cherry, you come back and tell me you wouldn't ride that beast!" She laughs, I shove her and laugh too.

I stir my drink with my straw, my mind wanders to that office and what exactly is going on in there. Why do I even care? I've known the guy a couple of days and it's clear he really isn't my type. Yes, he's fit, he's got all the assets that would break down the will power of the strongest feminist going, but he's a total pig.

Every time I see him, he's got a different girl on his arm and he makes no secret of the fact that he's willing to sleep with them. He's not the type of guy that's going to be tamed and certainly not the type of guy that's worthy of my virginity.

My thoughts are interrupted by a screech. Aria is wrapping Jack and his handsome boyfriend Beck, into a tight hug. Jack drags me towards them and we all end up in a group hug.

"So, what the hell is going on Bells?" asks Jack as we head to a booth. "You're not with Carl, you're with Carl, you're not with him, he breaks your face again, and then there's some hot god like creature trying to get in your pants?"

I glare at Aria who has clearly been gossiping, "He is not trying to get in my pants!" I protest.

"She wishes," grins Aria. "Wait till you see him guys, you will completely understand what I'm talking about."

"So, he doesn't want to get in your pants?" asks Beck looking confused. "Then who is he and what does he want? Men don't help a girl out if there's nothing in it for them Bells, we really are quite selfish like that!"

I shrug, I wonder the same thing, and no one can be that hot and nice, yet still single.

"He's just a nice guy. I'm not stupid though, and I'm pretty sure there's more to it, but for now I'm happy to have his help, so I'm just going along with it. He doesn't want me like that, he's got a different woman on his arm every night and he doesn't hide that from me, that's not the actions of a man trying to woo a girl." I finish my drink. "Let's go and dance, I don't want to talk about men anymore."

We spend the next hour laughing like loons and dancing. It feels like any normal night out before I found out that Dad had betrayed me. If I don't think about it, I almost forget. Then when I remember it's like I've been punched, and I find myself looking around at every scary looking man to see if I'm being watched.

As if feeling eyes on me, I glance around, and JP appears. As scary as he looks, he's a good-looking man and I find myself smiling.

"Bella, the boss is wondering where you are," he says into my ear.

The music is pounding. I look up to the balcony where the VIP area is and see him watching me. A drink in his hand.

"Well now he knows." I smile nodding towards him.

"I think he would prefer you in the VIP section where he knows you're safe," he explains.

I fling my arms around JP's neck. "Why don't you stay here and then I'm totally safe?" I make the suggestion with a wiggle of my hips. He holds me by the waist at arm's length, as if avoiding any body contact.

"Are you trying to get my ass kicked?" he grins, and I shrug. A smirk playing on my lips.

"Why would you get your ass kicked? It's not like he has any interest in me."

He shakes his head, laughing. "If only you knew!"

CHAPTER SIX

Aiden

I can't take my eyes off her, the way she dances and laughs with her friends has me intrigued. She is trying desperately to dance with JP and I know he's only holding back because I'm watching. It's a good thing I didn't send Raff to find her because he would do anything to annoy me.

She gives up on JP and leaves Aria talking to him. She turns her attention to a group of guys that have been dancing near her for the last ten minutes. I watch as one of the guys wraps his arms around her waist and she proceeds to dance with him, grinding herself into him.

I grip my drink a bit tighter. I can't storm down there and freak her out. I'm not meant to be showing interest in her to reel her in, but fuck if it isn't a struggle. I take some deep breaths trying to calm my inner cave man but then I see him lean towards her and it's like I lose all control and storm towards the stairs.

JP sees me heading in their direction and intercepts me. "Calm your shit down brother."

I glare at him knowing he's right. "Raff said earlier that I should try being myself, to be that possessive bastard because she might like it."

He drops his head and shrugs, then steps to one side as if he's given up trying to reason with my psycho side.

I press myself up against her back and she freezes, goose bumps rise on her arms.

"Are you trying to piss me off?" I growl in her ear. The guy she was dancing with steps back, he must recognize me.

"Why would I be pissing you off Aiden?" she asks innocently, and I'm not sure if she's playing her own game.

She presses her ass against me, and I suck in a breath, god she feels good against me. Flashes of her naked body flick through my mind.

"I warned you before what would happen if you keep rubbing up on me!"

She lays her head back against me and I instinctively

wrap my arms tighter around her. We stay like this for a while, enjoying each other's warmth. It's been a while since I've let anyone stay in my arms this long. Laying with her last night without even having sex was another first for me. *What is this girl doing to me?* Jake has got a lot to answer for.

Bella

I find myself warming to Aiden, his arms feel good around me, his six-foot-seven frame flanks my five-three and I feel safe here like this. I wonder what it would be like to be with him, to sleep with him. My thoughts are interrupted when he releases me and takes my hand, leading me from the dance floor and back to the VIP area.

He gets us a drink and we sit in his booth.

"Where did your friends go?" I'm referring to his little threesome show earlier. He eyes me suspiciously and takes a sip of his whiskey.

"I have no idea, I'm not the kind of guy to care about afterwards, I get what I need and then they leave."

I try not to look bothered by that confession. I feel like he's waiting for my reaction, but it's not like I didn't expect it. I've never seen him with the same woman more than once.

"Doesn't that get boring?"

He shrugs. "A man has needs. If they are met what's there to be bored with?"

"There's not much affection in that though, and

everyone likes a bit of affection, someone that cares."

"Not me sweetheart, all that fairy tale shit is for weak minded men that get married and trapped into the same routine."

"So, you've never had a girlfriend or anything more than a one-night stand?"

"I didn't say that did I? But I realized pretty quickly that relationships aren't for me. For one, I love sex way too much. You get into a relationship and it becomes about feelings and cuddles and less about the sex, and secondly, I'm too dominant. I like things done when I say and how I say. I'm too jealous and out of control," he admits.

"So, love makes you lose control? You don't like to feel out of control?"

"Exactly, so I avoid it. I have enough friends to hang with, male and female. Then I have women that I sleep with, keeping the two separate makes my life easier."

I've officially been friend zoned. I don't know why I feel disappointed when he's just admitted that he runs from everything that I run towards.

"So, you have Raff and JP? They are good friends?"

He nods with a grin. "They have known me my whole life, my mum said it felt like she had four kids instead of two."

"You have a brother or a sister?" I ask.

His eyes cloud slightly, and he fidgets. "A brother, he died."

I instinctively reach for his hand and place mine over it.

"That's awful Aiden, that must have been really hard on you all being so close." He nods and pulls his hand away taking another drink and then signaling for the bartender to bring another.

"So, how did you end up with Carl?" he asks changing the subject. He clearly doesn't like to talk about his brother.

"Erm, I met him in Costa, he asked me out. I thought it was love at first sight, but he turned out to be a dick so here I am," I tell him the quick version to make me look less pathetic.

"And he hits you often?" he asks.

"Just twice. We were always quite fiery and would often argue. People have had to separate us, but he's hit me twice, the time before this," I point to my bruised face, "was a month or so ago and I ended up in the hospital."

"And was that because you went out and ended up sleeping in a stranger's bed?" he jokes.

"No! I never do that. He wants me to sleep with him, but he comes on too strong, yah know? The harder he tries, the more I pull away. I don't want it to be a big deal, but I want to like the person I sleep with and I don't like him very much."

Aiden hands me a shot from the bottle of Sambuca he has at the table.

"I admire you. Not many women get to your age and are still virgins. Takes some will power to hold out until twenty-three."

"How do you know my age?" I ask confused. I drink the shot.

He knocks his back. "You told me," he says, but I know I didn't. Weird.

"Shall we head home?" he asks, pulling his phone out and swiping the screen.

"Yeah, I will go and let Aria know I'm off," he doesn't respond. Something has grabbed his attention on his phone.

When I get back to the booth Aiden is nowhere to be found but Raff is leaning against the table on his phone.

He looks pissed. "Got it, but you're gon fuck this up," he grates out hanging up the call.

"Hey baby girl, Aiden had to leave. He asked me to drop you home." I push the pang of disappointment down. I felt like we were connecting tonight and I'm not ready for the night to end yet.

"I can make my own way Raff, you stay and carry on working." I smile turning away from him, heading for the stairs.

"No Bella, Aiden was very clear that I take you back. He will want to know you're safe."

I frown at him. I don't like being told what to do, I never have, it makes me rebel more.

"Stop being weird Raff. I said no, I am fine. Now get

back to doing whatever it is you do." I say as I head for the exit.

Raff follows me, I know this because people are staring as I pass and that only ever happens if I'm with one of the guys. They command attention everywhere they go.

I get outside and the fresh air hits me. "Please Bella, let me drop you back home. Aiden will have my balls," he begs. I roll my eyes in frustration.

"Call him," I say, and Raff looks taken back.

"What?" he asks.

"I don't have his number, ring him and give me your phone." He does it reluctantly and hands me his mobile.

"Raff this better be good," snaps Aiden.

"If you're going to ditch me then at least stick around to say goodbye, and for the record, I don't need chaperoning anywhere so please tell your bull dog to back the fuck off!" I hand the phone back to Raff before stomping off down the street.

What is wrong with him? He can't just tell me what to do. I know he's doing me a favor letting me stay at his place, but to be fair I didn't ask him for that, he demanded it. We aren't in a relationship, he's made that very clear, so he needs to learn that if we are going to be friends then I won't be told what to do.

I spot a quiet little bar, the kind with low lighting and a soul singer in the corner. I decide to hide in there for a bit. I don't feel like heading back just yet, it will do him good to not get his own way. I feel like that doesn't happen where Aiden's concerned.

I order a glass of wine and take a seat at the back of the bar. Pulling out my phone, I spend some time catching up on my social media account. I search Aiden's name and his profile pops up. His profile picture is of him looking happy. I haven't known him long, but I've never seen his eyes shine like that.

The shrill ring of my phone makes me jump and I almost drop it. I don't recognize the number, so I swipe ignore and carry on with my Facebook stalking. His profile is set to private except for the picture he shared earlier of me and him. There are ten comments on the picture, so I open them. Most are from guys telling Aiden he is punching above his weight which makes me laugh. *As if, more like I am.*

There's one from Laurie Casey. I study the tiny profile picture next to her comment, she's stunning, blond, and just by her picture I can tell she's well put together. The kind of girl that looks flawless without phone filters.

"Hope this isn't your way of announcing you're in a new relationship, plastering across Facebook. How classy NOT!" It seems like this Laurie isn't happy with seeing Aiden in bed next to me.

"Call me," is Aiden's response to her catty comment. I wonder if she did call him and I wonder what she is to Aiden.

My phone flashes again with the same phone number calling me. I decide to answer it in case it's urgent. As soon as I place it to my ear, I know it's Aiden.

"Where the hell are you?" he yells. I disconnect the call. I am not answering to him, especially when he yells at me like that.

Aiden

I run my hands through my hair in anger. How dare she hang up on me. Who the hell does she think she is? I call Raff again to see if he's managed to find her yet.

"Aid, I don't get why you're stressing. We know she isn't in danger, no one paid her Dad remember?" he say's sounding annoyed.

I know what he's saying makes sense. She isn't in any danger, but I have to play the bastard part. She needs to think I care. Besides, I have this need to know that she's okay and where she is, even though I have no rights over her.

"Boss you're going to that dark place again, maybe all this is not a good idea."

I disconnect his call. I need to get a grip on this obsessive behavior before I lose it.

The door opens, and Laurie stands there in a silk night dress, short, just how I like them. Suddenly, I feel like this isn't where I need to be.

"Thought you'd never get here," she sighs, opening the door wider. I hesitate for a second and I see the annoyance in her expression. "Somewhere more important to be Aiden?"

I sigh and shake my head, "No princess." I head inside, already hating myself for giving in to her again.

I look around the hotel room, noticing she's already ordered me a bottle of my favorite whiskey. She sits on the edge of the bed.

"So, who is she?"

I bite my tongue in annoyance, "Nobody important Laurie."

She runs her hands along the hem of her night dress pouting. "You never post pictures on Facebook."

I roll my eyes as I crawl onto the bed, placing my hands either side of her, she lays back.

"Are we really going to waste time talking about unimportant shit or are we gon fuck?"

She places her hands above her head and I pull my tie off and use it to bind her hands.

"And stop Facebook stalking me, you're married!" I nip the top of her breast and she arches up, smiling.

"Then don't post pictures of you in bed with other

women, how would you feel if I posted pictures of me and other men?"

I crawl over her body until I'm sitting over her chest. I lift her head, lining her mouth up with my erection. "Laurie, it doesn't bother me. You shouldn't care what I think, worry about what your husband thinks!"

When she opens her mouth to speak, I press forward, my cock filling her mouth and touching the back of her throat. She takes it all, her eyes watering as I fuck her mouth. It doesn't take me long before I'm almost ready to release in her. All the build up with Bella has me in knots. I pull out and Laurie gasps for breath.

"Fuck, what's gotten into you Aiden?"

"Don't pretend you don't like it how I give it Laurie," I grin, tapping her ass to turn over. She does so without protest, sticking her ass up in the air. "It's the reason you call, so I can use you, fuck you," I push in to her tight pussy. "Do all the things that he doesn't do, the things you don't tell him you like in case he dumps your trashy ass." I coat my cock in her juices and then line it with her ass. I push forward and she lets out a deep, low moan.

"And does she let you do all this shit to her Aiden?" she pants, looking back at me over her shoulder. I grip the back of her neck, forcing her head to look forward and then I push her face in to the pillows. Holding her down while I fuck her hard and fast.

"You just concentrate on pleasing me, don't worry about what anyone else does for me."

CHAPTER SEVEN

Bella

I finally stumble my way into Tremos, the nightclub that Aiden lives above. JP is behind the main bar and I lean over the bar, so he can hear me.

"Large white wine please JP."

He hands me the glass. "Where's Aiden?" he asks, and I shrug.

Why does everyone treat me like his damn keeper?

A guy to my left catches my eye and smiles, I return the smile. He shuffles towards me.

"Hi, I'm Luke." He offers me his hand and I shake it, laughing at the formality.

We start talking and after an hour he's cheered me up. He's very funny and has many tales about his days as a student before he became a college professor. I missed out on those days because despite me leaving school with outstanding grades, I had to get a job to help support Dad.

The door man interrupts us, indicating that we need to drink up. I notice the lights have come on which means it must be at least three in the morning.

I've had such a good time with Luke that I'm not ready to say goodbye yet.

"Why don't we grab a coffee? I know a little all-night café just around the corner."

He smiles. "Sounds great, lead the way." I stand, and JP appears.

"Bells where are you off?" I give him my best *'what the hell does it have to do with you'* look. "JP I am a grown up, I don't need to get permission to leave the club."

"You don't even know this guy," he says rudely, nodding towards Luke. I take Luke's hand and lead him out of the club trying to hide my annoyance at all these bossy men that have recently appeared in my life.

We settle at the back of the café. "Who was that guy back at the club?" asks Luke.

"Would you believe me if I told you I actually don't know him that well? I'm staying with his friend temporarily, he's helping me out."

Luke blows out a breath. "Well he's a big guy, I don't want to piss him off if he's looking out for his mate."

"Trust me, his friend has no interest in me. We are friends and new friends at that," I reassure him.

"Good because I'd like to go out with you again some time, if you're available, that is?"

I smile and nod, "I am definitely available." I hand him my phone, "Put your number in and I will call you, so you have my number."

Once he hands my phone back to me it lights up with Aiden's number. I ignore it, I really don't want to hear his yelling.

I call Luke and he saves my number into his phone. He walks me back to the club and gives me a light kiss on the cheek. I like him, and I like that he doesn't try and stick his tongue down my throat.

I'm smiling as I enter the side door that leads into the club. The place is now empty of clubbers and I pass some of the bar staff that are heading home. I head to the bar where JP and Raff are chatting, while JP restocks the fridges. Raff sees me and whistles loud. I realize why, when Aiden storms from his office straight towards me. He looks so angry that my step falters.

"WHERE THE FUCK HAVE YOU BEEN?" he yells, not stopping until he's right in my face. I take a step back, he makes me feel uneasy when he's so angry like this and it reminds me of how little I know him.

"I've been out Aiden. What's the problem?"

He throws his hands in the air and turns to Raff and JP. "Is she for real?" he asks them and then turns back to me. "The problem is Bella, your Dad tried to fucking sell you to some nut jobs and then you stroll around like that's not an issue. Not only that, but you head out with some jumped up twat that you don't even know."

"I don't know you!" I yelled in outrage. "I don't know Raff or JP!"

"Then maybe you should get your head out of your ass and sort your life out. You're gullible and too trusting. I know all that and I've only known you a few days. If I know that then other men will pick up on that. No wonder you end up with assholes that hit you!"

I clench my fists and blink away the tears that suddenly rush to my eyes. I don't respond because I don't want him to know that he's hurt my feelings.

I head straight for the lift. I press the button a few times, it's taking forever to come.

"Come on damn it," I say to myself.

"I'm sorry Isabella, that was out of order," he says quietly from behind me.

"You are right though Aiden. I'm going to get my stuff and get out of your hair," I say, keeping my back to him.

The lift opens, and he follows me into it. I really need to cry but I hold it in because I can feel him staring at me.

"Don't go, please," he says and I turn to look at him.

"You don't owe me anything. I'm going back home and if someone turns up to claim me, I will call the police. It's not like it's legal to just sell your daughter's virginity," I joke with a small smile. "The whole weekend has been a bit crazy."

He nods his head. "It certainly has. I'd prefer you to stay tonight at least." The lift opens, and I follow him out. "Just sleep on it."

Aiden

I take her a bottle of water. She's curled up on my sofa and I note how good she looks there, like she belongs. I need to make this work, not just for me but for Raff and JP too. The clubs are our life, we have all put so much into them. Damn Jake and his stupid pranks, even in death he haunts me.

She sips the water and I sit next to her. I've removed my shirt, I know she likes what she sees because I keep catching her looking.

"You have so many tattoos," she says, looking over my chest. I don't have any skin left from my arms, chest and back because the whole thing is a canvas of various art work that Jake designed over the years. He was an amazing artist.

"My brother designed them all, there's pretty much one for anything big that's happened in our lives." I smile looking down at the different designs.

"Did he own the club with you?" she asks.

"Yeah, we were partners in all the businesses."

"You must miss him so much, having the clubs being

a constant reminder," she says sadly. If only she knew.

"I know your weirded out by me just turning up in your life, I've been a bit full on." I feel like I need to give her something if I want to pull her in and earn her trust.

"There's something about you, I'm just pulled towards you. Do you feel it too?" If the guys could hear me now, they would kick my ass. I'm not known for being corny.

"I feel an attraction Aiden," she admits, which surprises me. "But I know you're not into me like that and I'm not a one-night stand kind of girl, so let's work on being friends. I think having a possessive male friend might do me good, maybe you can help me be less gullible?" she asks, arching her eyebrow. I nod, at least she is happy for me to remain in her life, now I just need to make her want to sleep with me!

Bella

I lay on the sofa, it's so comfy that I had no problem arguing that I wanted to sleep here so Aiden could keep his bed. He has a spare room but there's no bed in it. He said he is getting me one, but I told him I really didn't want him to go to any trouble. I don't expect to be here that long anyway. Aiden said he's sorting out my Dad's mess, whatever that means.

My phone lights up and I smile when I see it's Luke telling me what a good night he had. He wants to meet for a drink after work on Monday. I type a quick reply saying I would love that, and he arranges to meet me from work at five.

I wake to hear crashing and banging coming from the kitchen area. I open one eye and spot Aiden in running shorts and a vest looking hot and sweaty.

"Sorry did I wake you?" he whispers.

I smile, "It's your house, make as much noise as you want."

He stands in front of me stretching out the muscles in his legs. I try not to check out his hot body and the fact that he looks amazing dripping in sweat. He grins, letting me know that he's caught me looking and I pull the pillow over my head groaning.

"It should be illegal to look like that."

He laughs. "It takes a lot of hard work to look like this. Early morning runs are not fun on a Sunday morning."

I sit up and pull the covers around me.

"What are your plans today?" he asks wiping his chest with a hand towel.

"I might go to the gym and then maybe see if I can get a wax and my nails done." My friend has her own salon which she opens exclusively for her friends on a Sunday, so I often get a spray tan and nails.

"Wax?" he wiggles his eyebrows and I smile.

"Well I have a date tomorrow and I don't want hairy legs scaring him away." His face drops and he looks annoyed.

"A date?" he repeats.

"Yeah, a guy I met last night. Only for a drink after work but still, I have to make a bit of an effort, don't I?"

He heads to his bedroom without a word and I'm left wondering what I did wrong this time.

Aiden

I need to make a move sooner than planned. I need to be in her head all the time, so she doesn't arrange stupid dates with other men. I call in a few favors and then head back to the living room where Bella sat smiling at her phone.

"Get dressed we are going out."

She looks up from her phone. "Aiden what are you talking about?"

"We are going bedroom shopping. I have a friend who owns a furniture place, she's opening just for us today, so we can get your room sorted," I explain.

"I'm going to be here for a short time, I don't need a bedroom and I can't afford to furnish one even if I wanted to," she argues.

"Time is ticking, get dressed," I repeat, ignoring her argument.

I can feel her looking at me nervously as I swing the car into Bond Street. I pull up outside Harpers' store. Her furniture is exclusive and costs a fortune, but I know Bella will love it.

She gets out of the car warily and looks around at all the expensive shops surrounding us.

"Aiden I can't afford anything on Bond Street." I take her hand and pull her into the shop.

Harper greets us with a huge smile. She is stunning and was madly in love with my brother, Jake. He met her after his diagnosis, so refused to get involved with her. He didn't want to make her fall in love with him only to leave her behind. She fell anyway, and she is still very much heartbroken.

"Aiden," she smiles kissing each cheek, "and this must be Isabella?" she adds kissing her too. "Take your time, give me a shout if you see anything you like. My guy already has his van out the back with the bed in, so we can just add to that." I nod and smile at Bella who looks like a deer caught in head lights. It's very obvious that she isn't used to having money, which is a quality that I love about her.

Once Harper has returned to her seat at the front desk, I turn to Bella.

"Look, you're doing me a favor Bella, I need the

spare room furnishing and I want a woman's touch so think of it as helping a friend out."

She sighs and then gives a nod. "Fine, I guess I can help a friend out."

CHAPTER EIGHT

Aiden

We spend over an hour picking out bedside tables, lamps, cushions, blankets and various other chick bits that Bella insists will look amazing. If I'm honest, I hate shopping but being here with Bella has been fun. We have laughed, and I've really enjoyed being with her. Once I settled the bill we head outside.

"I would really love to take you to lunch," I say. "A thank you for all of your help."

"Well as long as you know this isn't a date Aiden. I really don't want it to be awkward when I have to turn you down." She smirks.

I smile and grab her hand, something I seem to do automatically and without much thought.

"You wish lady," I say, dragging her across the street.

We take a short walk until I find a quiet little Italian restaurant. The owner knows me here, so I know we will be offered a table, even though it's usually very busy. I'm right, Lucas takes us straight to a table at the back where it's a bit quieter.

"I'm impressed Aiden, shops that open at your request, lunch in popular, booked up restaurants where the owner clearly thinks highly of you, remind me why you're single again?" I pour some more wine into her glass.

"Because that's the way I like it," I remind her. Her smile falters but she soon recovers and sips her wine.

"I don't blame you, I'm thinking single life is the way forward."

I give a small laugh, "Does your Monday evening date know this?"

"Luke seems like a nice guy, but I always think that. I can't help but think that maybe I just need to get rid of it, yah know? I'm being too fussy."

I almost choke on my water. "Get rid of what?" I know exactly what she's going to say. She wants to get rid of her virginity to some random guy.

"You know what I mean," she says, and when I don't respond she leans in closer, "My virginity."

I raise my eyebrows. "Why wait all this time just to give it away to some random?"

She fiddles with her fork. "I told you, I haven't been holding on for some special guy, it just happened this way. Once it came to it I could never quite do it, but now it feels like a burden."

The lunch arrives, and we eat in silence. Eventually she places her fork down. "I read in a magazine once about a girl that sold her virginity to a millionaire." I actually choke on my steak and she hands me a napkin laughing. "It's a real thing!" she nods.

"Bella stop," I sigh, "It's not a burden. You have waited this long, don't just sleep with anyone and please don't prostitute yourself." She looks embarrassed and blushes slightly. "Besides, if you really want to give it up, I can sort out that problem for you." I wink, and she blushes a deeper red.

"I wouldn't want to break your heart once I've used you," she smiles, and I laugh. "Thanks for today Aiden, it's been fun."

"It's not over yet," I say, "we have a room to set up."

Bella

I flop onto the sofa next to JP. "I am so tired," I yawn. He slaps my thigh.

"Well at least you have a bedroom now."

The guys came over along with Aria and we spent the entire afternoon fixing my room.

Aiden ordered a huge Oak bed with the most comfortable mattress, it looks cozy with the cottage style décor I chose today.

We are all huddled around the coffee table, sitting on the floor eating Chinese take-out. I've known these guys a few days, but I feel like I've known them forever. We laugh and joke, and I feel like we have really hit it off.

Once the guys leave, me and Aiden decide to watch a horror film, even though I hate horrors. I spend most of the time hiding behind him, which I think he secretly enjoys. My cheeks hurt from all the laughing today and I can't remember a time when I was so happy and care free. When my time comes to an end with Aiden, I hope we remain friends because I'd hate to not be around him ever again.

The next morning, I arrive at the shop ready to bake my happy heart out. Aria is already there whipping up some muffins and I join her at the counter, tying my apron.

"I think I am totally in love with Raff. He is the perfect guy for me." I roll my eyes because Aria has said this at least a hundred times before. "Don't roll your eyes Bells, he was made for me, he just doesn't know it yet. And don't think I don't see the way you and lover boy look at each other." I fain innocence.

"We are friends, he doesn't have relationships and I require more than one night."

"Bella, give him one night and he will be hooked," she suggests.

"I'm not risking my heart for him to break it, which he will and we both know it. That's why I'm meeting Luke after work."

She drops the spoon in her bowl of mixture. "Oh Bella, he sounds boring, Mr. Safe and Reliable."

I glare at her open mouthed. "You don't even know him, he's very good looking and he makes me laugh," I defend him.

"But does he set you on fire with his touch like Aiden?" she asks, and I chuck a cloth at her.

"Not everything is about sex Ari, the sooner you realize that, the quicker you will find Mr. Right."

It's been a busy day and I'm dead on my feet, but I smile when the bell rings and I see Luke walk through the door.

"Hey," he grins.

"Mr. Boring has arrived," whispers Aria in my ear. I elbow her, and she giggles handing me my jacket.

"Aria meet Luke, Luke this is my very annoying friend and boss, Aria." I smile.

He shakes her hand and she frowns at his hand shake. When he turns away to look around the shop, she's still holding her hand out in front of her staring at it, she turns to me and mouths *"What the fuck?"* like no one's ever shaken her hand before. I grin and shove her.

The bell goes again, and I look up to see Aiden standing there. He glares at Luke and then turns to me.

"Bella, I know you're out tonight, but I really need

you." His eyes tell me that he's upset about something and I go straight to him. "What's happened?"

"I need a favor, I wouldn't ask if it wasn't really important."

I look to Luke who nods, "You go Bella, we can do drinks another night," he kisses my cheek. "I will text you later."

After he's gone, Aiden rolls his eyes and I catch Aria doing the same, "What?"

"He's too nice," says Aria and Aiden nods in agreement.

"How can someone be too nice Aria? He's a gentleman."

"All I know is that if some guy came and interrupted my date with you, I wouldn't have been the one leaving," says Aiden.

He takes my hand and pulls me to his car. I notice his mood seems to have lifted, he doesn't look so upset anymore.

We pull up outside a posh looking bar. There are lots of people inside and Aiden turns to me.

"I need you to pretend to be my date."

I can't believe him, I am so mad. "What do you mean? Aiden, have you just ruined my date so you can use me?"

He shrugs and gives me an unapologetic smile. "It's a desperate situation and what's the point in me having a female friend if I can't use her?"

"Aiden that's not cool and anyway, I'm not dressed for this," I say, pointing towards the bar.

He points to the back seat. "Blacked out windows, no one can see," he says, and I look into the back seat to see a box, which I already know will contain an outfit.

I sigh and glare at him.

"Come on Bells, you owe me," he grins, and I know he's right. Without him I'd have nowhere to stay. I climb into the back and he turns to watch me.

"Really? Turn around." He laughs and turns back to face the front.

"Yah know, I've already seen you completely naked when you tried to seduce me but fell to sleep in my bed." I groan with embarrassment.

"I cannot be responsible for what the drunk me does Aiden, it's something you need to know if you're going to continue to be my friend."

I struggle into the tight black dress and add the heels that are way higher than I'm used to. I add a touch of mascara and some red lipstick.

"I'm ready. What exactly are we doing here?"

He opens my car door and takes my hand, helping me out. "You just need to pretend to be my date, if anyone asks. It's early days but we are happy, and you are not in the spare room."

"Why would anyone ask that?"

"Oh trust me, they will," he mutters, leading me inside.

Its busy and everyone is drinking champagne and chatting about business and important adult stuff. I am bored, and I don't know how to speak to these people. I feel uncomfortable and Aiden keeps dragging me from group to group.

I leave him chatting with a group of bar owners and head to the toilet. I'm touching up my makeup when the blond that I instantly recognize from his Facebook, appears next to me.

She glances across to me in the mirror then begins touching up her own makeup.

"So, you and Aiden?" she asks. "He never mentioned you."

I run my fingers through my hair. "Should he have?"

She slowly pops her things back in her clutch bag, "Depends how long you have been together sweet heart because he fucked me on Saturday night!"

I watch open mouthed as she waltzes out, I stand for a minute gathering myself. It shouldn't bother me because me and Aiden aren't together and it's not like I don't know that he sleeps around. It feels like she's chucked ice cold water on me.

I give my shoulders a shake to relax them and lift my chin. I've got to stop thinking that Aiden's going to fall madly in love with me or I'm going to end up with a broken heart and it will be my own doing.

Aiden is waiting for me near by the toilet. "Bella, I need to introduce you to a lawyer that I know. It's very important that you help me convince him that we are together and totally falling in love." I smile and nod, "Are you okay?" he queries, a look of concern on his face.

"Yeah of course show me the way." I force a smile.

"Isabella, this is a good friend of mine, Drake. He's a solicitor," says Aiden.

I smile at the tall, thin man. He looks older than Aiden, but I feel like he's around the same age.

"Lovely to finally meet you Isabella, Aiden has told me so much about you." he smiles shaking my hand. I raise my eyebrow at Aiden who looks uncomfortable.

"All good things I hope?" He nods.

We are interrupted when the blond bitch taps Aiden on the shoulder. He closes his eyes briefly like he's annoyed, but he lets her link her arm in his.

"Walk with me Aiden." He turns to me and Drake and gives an apologetic smile.

"Can you excuse me for a minute, I'll be right back."

Blondie smirks and leads him away and I am left glaring at his back in disgust. He dragged me here, tells me to lie to everyone then just leaves me with some stranger to convince him of our love, how am I supposed to do that when he's left me, so he can go and talk to another woman. They disappear towards the toilets and I turn back to Drake with a shrug, "Must be important."

CHAPTER NINE

Aiden

"What is so urgent that you have to fuck up my plans tonight?" Laurie leads me upstairs towards the toilets. We bypass them, and she opens some double doors that lead onto a roof terrace. She closes them behind her. The roof terraced is closed to the public tonight as it's a private function. We stand looking over the edge at the busy streets below.

"I text you and you didn't reply yesterday," she pouts, "I think he's having an affair."

I roll my eyes in annoyance. "So are you Laurie." She rubs her hands up and down my arms.

"Don't be cross with me baby, you know you're more than just an affair," she soothes kissing my cheek. I don't look at her, my weakness for her will crack if I look at her. I know she's wearing red and I'm a sucker for it, as she well knows.

"Look at me Aiden," she whispers, and I turn my head slightly. She kisses the corner of my mouth and I don't move away, giving her the green light to take the kiss deeper.

She's wriggled her way in front of me and she is now trapped between me and the balcony wall. I feel her rub against me and I groan. I know I'm being weak but there's something about her that has me forgetting how to say no.

"You can't stay mad at me for long baby," she pants rubbing my cock through my trousers. She makes quick work of undoing my button and tugs my trousers down just enough to free me. "I forgot to put on my knickers tonight," she whispers seductively into my ear.

I lift her long red dress, bunching it around her waist. It's an automatic action, like my hands have a mind of their own whenever she is around me.

I lift her, and she wraps her legs around my hips, like she's done a thousand times before.

I swallow her scream as I push my cock straight in, not checking if she's ready. She's panting and moaning, spurring me to move quicker. I push harder until I feel like I've filled her all the way.

She digs her nails into my back, the pain giving me

the extra thrill. I grip the balcony edge, giving myself more leverage to pound into her. I use my free hand to pull down her dress, her breasts swelling as the cold air hits them. I take the nearest one into my mouth and she lets out a scream. I'm breathless, her pussy grips me tighter as I move faster and faster. I finally feel her shake, squeezing my cock harder and I let my release go on a roar.

I press my face into her neck, taking a minute to get my breath back. She drops her legs back to the ground and tucks me back into my trousers and fastens my button.

"I think she likes to watch you," she whispers into my ear, slowly running her tongue up my neck. It takes a second to realize what she's saying but when it clicks, my head shoots up and Bella is standing at the doors, tears in her eyes.

"Fuck!"

Bella

"Fuck," I hear him yell as I turn and run back towards the stairs.

Why would he bring me here and make me cancel my date to go and have sex with her? It's so disrespectful and seedy. I'm crying out of anger and maybe a small piece of heart break that I have no right to.

I shove the doors open, almost knocking into a doorman, and head for the tube. It begins to rain.

"Marvelous," I shout up towards the sky. I don't even have my jacket, it's in his car.

My phone buzzes in my bag and I stop to pull it out. Of course it's Aiden, so I cancel the call, but it immediately lights up again. I shove it back in my bag and look around at my surroundings. I decide to go into a busy bar and head straight for the toilet. The rain is coming down hard and I need to get shelter. I take out my phone and I have five missed calls from him. As if he senses it's in my hand, he rings again.

I connect the call but I don't speak. I leave that up to him.

"Bella, where are you, it's raining, you don't have a coat, let me come and get you!" He's shouting over the rain and traffic, so I know he's out looking for me.

"Why did you do that to me tonight Aiden," I ask, hurt evident in my voice, "Why did you make me cancel on my date?"

"Cos' it's what I do Bella, I screw up all of the time, please let me get you so I can talk to you," he begs.

"I don't want to talk, you humiliated me tonight, you're supposed to be my friend."

The toilet door flies open, and I'm shocked to see Aiden standing there. Phone to his ear. His hair is dripping from the rain, He looks sexy as hell.

"I'm sorry," he whispers into the phone. His eyes staring directly into mine. I cancel the call without breaking eye contact.

"You hurt my feelings tonight, don't ever do that again."

He stuffs his phone into his pocket and puts his hand out towards me. "Let's go home Bells." I fold my arms across my chest and march past him.

"I'm not touching you when you've been touching her!" I head out into the rain with him hot on my heels.

Aiden

"Jesus Aiden, what is it with you and that stuck up bitch?" snaps JP, slamming his hands on the bar. The club is quiet with it being a Monday, just a few business types dotted about.

Bella went straight up to the apartment when we arrived home five minutes ago. I've filled JP and Raff in on my disastrous night.
Tonight, was about proving to Drake that I had met Bella and things were going well. Then I fucked it up.

She didn't speak to me at all in the car and when I tried to apologize for the hundredth time she shrugged and smiled and told me not to worry about it, that I don't owe her anything and I'm free to fuck who I like. Then why do I feel so shit about the whole thing.

I knock my whiskey back. "I fucked up, what do you want me to say?" -Raff shakes his head in disgust- "What?"

"You're going to lose it all Aiden, you get that, right? Laurie dumped your ass for some rich dick and you're risking it all for her," Raff grates out, anger radiating off his huge shoulders.

"This is Jakes fault, stupid son of a bitch, I can't play this fucked up game." I pour another drink and swallow it back.

"Give up then," says JP, "Prove him right, you have always been a selfish bastard, why should we expect anything different!"

I watch him stomp off to the back room.

"It's not hard Aiden, fuck the virgin, most men would kill for that challenge," mutters Raff. I glance at him and shake my head.

"Why her though, why did Jake pick her?" I've asked the same question over and over. There's no obvious connection between them and the rules state that I can't reveal to her who he is, so I can't even ask outright. Raff slaps my back hard and I wince.

"Who cares, just get the job done Aiden so we can get on with our lives."

Bella

"I don't see your problem Bells, you aren't together," says Aria, giving me a confused look while she fills the glass cabinet in the window.

I came into work at five this morning because I couldn't sleep. Most of the baking was done before she even arrived.

I didn't see Aiden after I left him at the bar last night. I went straight to bed and even though I heard him come back to the apartment, mainly because he was stumbling about, I didn't go out to him. Aria is right, I have no claim to him, but it hurt anyway.

"I know Ari, but I cancelled my date, why didn't he just take her to the stupid thing?"

"No one likes a nag Bella, if you like him so much just sleep with him, I don't think he will turn you down, offer it as a business proposition," she grins. I roll my eyes.

"I'd rather not now I've seen the number of women he sleeps with."

"Hey, none of them will compare to a virgin," she

states, closing the cabinet.

"He doesn't deserve my virginity!"

She leans against the counter, "Was it hot?" She smirks, delight dancing in her eyes.

"What?" I ask confused, then realize what she's asking me and swat her with a towel.
"Aria Blotts, you are disgusting!" She laughs, and I turn towards the kitchen.

"It certainly haunted my dreams," I grin, glancing back at her. She lets out a little yell, "I knew it, he's too hot to be a shit lay!"

When I get home, the apartment is quiet. There're candles on the dining table and flowers. Oh great, just what I need, to be trapped in my room all night listening to his bloody date night. He appears by the table holding wine. I take in his jeans, clinging to his muscly thighs and the white t-shirt that shows off his big torso.

"I hope you haven't eaten?" he asks hopefully, and I shake my head. "It's my way of making up for your missed date night." he adds pulling out a seat. I lower myself into it.

"Aiden this isn't necessary, I flew off the handle last night, I must be getting my period or something."

He sits opposite me and lifts the lid from the large pot in the center of the table. It smells delicious. He spoons some into my bowl.

"Homemade soup," he says, placing it in front of me, "I can't take the credit, my mom helped me out."

I smile and have a taste. Leek and potato, one of my favorites and it's amazing.

"This is my first date," he says, "Even Laurie didn't get an official date out of me."

So, Laurie is a past girlfriend, the thought annoys me, but I smile.

"Lucky me!"

"I met her when I was 20," he carries on and even though I don't want to hear about her, I like that he's opening up to me. He doesn't seem the type. "I fell for her almost instantly, she just has this way of pulling the beast out of me, she goes above and beyond to push my boundaries. At first, I loved it, the chemistry we had was the best high I've ever experienced but it soon becomes too much when you spend every night being some jealous, raging hulk. She met someone else, he's rich and treats her better, well most of the time," he explains, "She's married. On her wedding day she fucked me in her hotel room, wearing her expensive dress and then I watched her marry him, getting off on the fact that I'd had her screaming my name an hour before she promised herself to him!" His confession makes me feel sick and I stop eating.

"Jake hated her, he said she had some spell over me, still does I guess but it pissed him off," he smiles at the memory, "Last night was wrong, I'm sorry I did that to you."

"You don't have to apologize, but I appreciate it Aiden. Laurie doesn't sound like a nice person. It sounds to me like she wants everything. It's not fair to keep you on speed dial when she's married but if she makes you happy then that's all that matters."

He nods thoughtfully. "I think she's a habit that I'm struggling to break."

"Maybe you need to say no to her a few times, stop

being at her beck and call?"-I stand- "Why don't we watch a film and forget about last night?"

We are halfway through Love Actually, much to Aiden's disgust. He's had a missed call from Laurie, and she's texted him, but he's ignored her, much to my delight; he listened to my advice.

His phone flashes again and he sighs.

"Answer it for me," he says, holding it to me.

"No way!"

"Please, maybe she will back off if she thinks you're here." I roll my eyes and take his phone.

"Hello."

"Put him on," she snaps, and I raise my eyebrows, rude.

"He's not available right now, can I take a message?" Aiden smiles at my posh accent.

"He is always available for me, tell him it's me!" Her clippie tone annoys me.

"I don't want to do that right now."

"Listen bitch, he is not going to be happy when he realizes you have answered his phone and that you're screening his calls. I suggest you get him now."

I release a low, rumbling moan, and Aiden raises his eye brows in surprise

"OOO baby, yes right there," I whisper, making her think that I am getting down an' dirty. "I'm not screening his calls Laurie, he is. And as I've already explained, he's not available right now because he's balls deep in me!"

I hang up laughing so much that tears roll down my face.

Aiden

She chucks the phone at me, her laugh making me smile.

"Oh my god I can't believe I just did that!"

I'm shocked and I daren't move in case she spots the fact that I am rock hard for her right now. What I wouldn't give to hear that moan while I am balls deep inside her.

She's still laughing and hasn't notice my uncomfortable fidgeting. She leans in and places her hand on my chest.

"I am so embarrassed," she giggles and before I even have time to think about what I'm doing, I kiss her. Just gentle, to the side of her mouth and then I pause, my hands either side of her face. I stare into her shocked eyes. Before she can protest, I decide I have to have at least one taste, I place another gentle kiss on her lips, she gasps, and I take the opportunity to kiss her deeper. I sweep my tongue into her mouth and grip the back of her neck, holding her close to me.

She tastes sweet and fresh, her eyes are closed, and I

feel her delicate hands grip my t-shirt, scrunching it up in her small fists.

I pull away but keep my hands in her hair. I stare into her blue eyes,

"Sorry, I couldn't help it," I whisper.

When she says nothing, I smile and pull back, enjoying the dumbfounded look on her face.

We are interrupted when her phone begins vibrating across the table. She gives a nervous cough and reaches for it.

The caller ID flashes Luke's name and I squeeze my hands into fists, great timing shit head.

She answers giving me a nervous look.

"Hey Luke." She goes quiet while he speaks to her. "Yeah sure, what time?"

I shake my head in annoyance, she had better not be arranging a date when she just let me stick my tongue down her throat.

"Okay, see you then." She hangs up.

"See him when?" I ask, and she looks at me; Chewing on her lower lip.

"Tomorrow."

I stand up glaring at her. "You're going on a date with him?" and she nods making the fire inside me rage. "You just let me fucking kiss you and then you arrange to meet Mr. Safe for a date!"

"Well you shouldn't have kissed me Aiden," she snaps "Friends don't do that. It's your fault I didn't go on the first date." I grab my phone and pull my trainers on. "Where are you going?" she asks as I head to the door with her hot on my heels. I turn on her and she comes to an abrupt stop.

"To see Laurie!" I growl and storm off, slamming the door behind me.

I arrive at the hotel. The guy behind the desk gives me a nod which means she's on her own. I slip him a twenty and head straight up to her room.

I shouldn't be here, but I'm angry and she can handle my rage. I bang on the door and it flies open. She stands there looking angry yet pleased.

My hand wraps around her throat and I push her backwards, kicking the door shut behind me.

She grins, "Please don't think you can come here when you have just left her bed." she spits angrily. I push her against the wall, my hand remains gripping her throat.

My heart is screaming at me to walk away, I know this isn't right, but I want to prove that Bella isn't affecting me, that I can override these feelings whirling around in my head.

"Are you serious about her?" she asks trying to remove my hand. I don't answer. I grip the top of her silk night dress and pull it hard. It rips instantly and falls to her feet.

She slaps me hard and I wince before gripping her hands and placing them above her head.

"She is nothing to me, I don't fuck virgins," I growl, kissing up her neck. I see the smug smile forming on her perfect face. I've never noticed how much make-up Laurie wears, I find It irritates me and Bella's flawless face flashes through my mind.

I close my eyes and grip Laurie's neck tighter. She gets a hand free and claws at my face, she smiles with satisfaction when she realizes she's drawn blood

I pull her leg up and wrap it around my waist. I fumble with my jeans, inching them down just enough to pull my hard cock free. My fist wraps in her hair and I pull her head to the side.

"You fucking bitch," I growl the words into her ear and she nips at my neck. I let her mark me, closing my eyes as she sucks at my skin.

I line my cock up to her entrance and she's panting, digging her nails into my back.

"Fuck me," she demands, wriggling. I push forward, and she screams my name. My movements are urgent and jerky, I can't get Bella out of my head, the thought of her tanned legs wrapped around me, her soft lips begging me to fuck her. It's not long before I explode, biting my tongue hard so I don't shout out Bella's name.

Laurie pushes down on my shoulders, she hasn't reached her orgasm yet. I let her guide me to my knees and place my mouth at her wet entrance. She puts her leg over my shoulder, hooking it behind my neck and pulling me to her. She grinds herself against my mouth, panting and pulling at my hair.

She stiffens, before screaming my name and I smile as I taste both of our orgasms on my tongue. She releases her grip and I stand, kissing my way up her toned skin.

She places her hand against the cheek she scratched, pulling it away and showing me the blood.

"Ouch," she smiles, licking it from her palm, "Clean up, I'll pour you a drink."

I stare into the mirror above the sink. I hardly notice the 3 scratches across my cheek, or the bite mark on my neck, because all I can see is guilt.

I splash my face and growl into my hands. Why can't I get her out of my head? I haven't even fucked her. I can imagine her disappointed face, hurt in her eyes and I want to put my fist through the mirror.

There's a tap on the door and Laurie enters, still naked. She has red marks around her neck and bruises to her hips where I gripped her. She stands in front of me so that she's leaning against the sink and hands me a bottle of whisky and places my mobile phone on the counter top. She watches me carefully as I swig straight from the bottle.

"I haven't seen you this distracted in a while," she muses running her finger nail down my front. I take another swig and she places her hand on my cock, gently gripping it.

"Who is this girl anyway?" she asks, licking up the side of my neck over the mark she put there earlier.

"A friend, I'm helping her out with accommodation." I close my eyes as she continues to rub me.

"She's living with you?" she queries, halting her movements. I cover her hand with my own and encourage her to continue.

"It's not a permanent thing, she's in the spare room." I groan, watching her well-manicured hand gripping my hard cock, I let my head fall back.

"And she's a virgin?" she asks. I nod rubbing my hands across her breasts, rolling her nipples between my thumb and forefinger.

"Why haven't you fucked her?"

"Cos' I want a woman that can handle me, not some quiet little virgin that has this ridiculous notion of love and saving herself, fuck that, I need experience and skill, she's a chick after a free ride," I say, leaning in to her and kissing her hard. She guides me back to her entrance, looking satisfied with my answer and I slowly sink into her, groaning with pleasure, all thoughts of guilt disappearing as I watch my cock disappear inside of her.

CHAPTER TEN

Bella

I replay the message, anger rushing through my veins. "Cos' I want a woman that can handle me, not some quiet little virgin that has this ridiculous notion of love and saving herself, fuck that, I need experience and skill, she's a chick after a free ride."

The smugness in his voice is not wasted on me. This is the second time I've heard him fuck her, so much for a one-night stand kind of guy.

I chuck my phone on my bed and decide to get ready for work.

He didn't come home last night and I'm glad. I would have shown him how quiet I can be right before I punched his smug bastard face.

Aria arrives, and I've already filled the cabinets in the window.

"I could get used to this," she smiles. "Two early starts in one week, what's he done now?"

I slide my phone across the table and she picks it up.

"Press play," I say, not taking my eyes off the icing I am adding to the cupcake in front of me. She presses play and I listen to the message for the hundredth time. Aria gasps and stares at me wide eyed.

"Shit Bells, talk about straight for the jugular."

"He is a complete and utter prick, I am so over him."

I called Aria last night and filled her in about the kiss. I actually swooned when I told her it was the most gentle and amazing kiss I'd ever had, stupid me.

When he left, I didn't think for one minute he would go to Laurie, I assumed he was just trying to hurt my feelings. I even cancelled my date with Luke, I only agreed in the first place because he'd caught me off guard when I was still on a high from Aiden's mind-blowing kiss.

When I woke during the night, I noticed a missed call from him and smiled when I saw he had left me a message, thinking he was apologizing for his jealous outburst.

I had smiled to myself when I'd pressed play. The smile soon disappeared when I realized it was him and Laurie talking on the message. I shouldn't let him bother me; I was naïve to think that a kiss meant anything more than just a kiss.

Aria talks me into having a night out with her and Jack, so we can dissect my sad life and make a plan.

When I get in from work, Aiden is sitting at the kitchen table working away on his laptop. He looks up and I notice angry scratches across his cheek. He doesn't speak, and I head straight for my room. I hope she scratched him because I answered his phone, bastard.

I decide to go girly for our drinks tonight and wear a short, white summer dress. It flows nicely around my curves and shows off my golden tan.

Aiden is watching television when I head back through the apartment.

"Date night?" he asks, not looking away from the TV.

"Actually no, I cancelled my date after you left last night." I slip on my sandals. He sits up and looks at me, I notice the bright red mark on his neck and it makes me feel sick. He catches me looking and pulls his collar up slightly, looking embarrassed.

"Well, do you want to do something?" he asks, and I laugh. I can't believe the nerve of the guy.

"Really Aiden?" He shifts uncomfortably. "You want to take me out with scratches across your face and a love bite marking your neck?"

"It's not what it looks like Bella," he mutters, not quite meeting my eye.

"Oh, so it's not that you turned to Laurie last night after you kissed me?" I ask doing my best to look surprised.

"No, not at all," he says standing up. I put my hand up to stop him approaching me.

"As I keep saying Aiden, you are a free man, you can see whoever you like but please don't lie to my face."

He puts his hands out and smiles, "Bella I'm not lying."

So, he's a big fat liar as well as a sex addicted, bastard. Note to self, never ever trust this man.

I turn and head for the door, he dives in front of me blocking my escape.

"We talked about you being out on the town with no

one to watch you, it's not safe," he tries. "Let me come, just to keep an eye on you."

"JP is already coming," I say, nice try asshole.
He sighs and rubs his forehead in frustration. "I keep fucking up Bella, I don't know how to do any of this."
I fold my arms, the action pushes up my breasts and his eyes are immediately drawn there. I roll my eyes and drop my arms back to my side. "I just want to go and meet my friends. JP said that the threat has died down so hopefully I will be out of your hair in no time."
His face drops, "JP said what?" His eyes flash with anger.

"Oh, and I've left some rent money on the side, I don't want you to think I'm after a free ride." I emphasize the last bit and smile. He looks confused but moves to the side so I can leave.

Aiden

As soon as the door closes, I call JP.

"Yeah man?" he answers.

"Why the fuck are you telling her the threat is almost over?"

"Because you're fucking it all up Aiden. I like the girl and I can't stand what you're doing. The clubs, the businesses, they don't mean shit if you're going to hurt an innocent girl like Bella."

"She was always going to get hurt JP; did you think I was going to sleep with her and marry her!" He goes silent and I wonder if he's with her now.

"Why do you have to be such a dick, you are letting a chance of happiness slip through your fingers, Your making a mess of it and I don't think this is what Jake meant," he hisses quietly, like he doesn't want to be over heard.

"No JP, you're risking everything because you want to bang her friend, you mess this up and I will tell Sara what you're up to while she's looking after your baby." It's a low blow but I'm pissed off.

JP and Sara aren't together, she fell pregnant after a one-night stand with him. She thinks the sun shines out of his ass. She wouldn't entertain his bed hopping if she knew he was following Aria around like a lost puppy dog.

"Fuck you Aiden," he growls, before disconnecting the call.

I feel like the shittiest friend, but I can't have him messing this up. He will forgive me, he knows I won't ring Sara, I'm just letting off some steam.

Bella

Seeing Aria all over JP guts me but I'm happy for my friend. Once she realized she wasn't getting anywhere with Raff, her attentions turned to poor JP. I want what she has, that confidence that will slay a man as he kisses her feet.

Jack sighs. "Bella, it sounds like a bad romance book." I nod.

"I know, right? I just need to move out, I've been flat hunting on the internet, Aria said she will lend me the deposit."

He holds my hand. "I think that's for the best, this guy's got heartbreak written all over him," he warns. "Have you had any dodgy men approach you about this deal your Dad supposedly made?"

I shake my head and stir my cocktail with my straw.

"No, it's weird, maybe Dad explained to them and sorted it out. JP seems to think I'm not in any real danger. If he's sold me to some fitty then maybe I will roll with it." I smile and Jack laughs.

I watch everyone else laughing and having fun. I find

my mind wondering to Aiden. I wish he was here, even though I hate him right now, I miss his attention and the way he makes me smile.

When JP suggests heading back to Tremos my heart rate spikes a little in the hope he will be around.

We arrive and Aiden is behind the bar, he looks odd there, out of place.

"Shit what happened to your face?" asks JP.

"I caught it," he says handing JP a pint. "Sorry about earlier," he adds, and JP fist bumps him.

"What did you catch it on?" asks Aria. "It looks like nail marks."

He wipes the bar top avoiding our stares.

"A cat." he shrugs, and I laugh at the audacity to continue his lies.

I pull out my phone and Jack laughs, knowing where this is going. I find the recording and place my phone on the bar.

"Press play when you're ready," I challenge him. He looks at me and then JP nervously.

"It's okay, I've got it," smiles Aria, leaning forward

and pressing play.

I let the recording play out, including the moans and groans that continue after his statement. He has the nerve to look pissed off and he stops the recording.

"I'd say those scratches were from a dog, not a cat," grins Aria handing my phone back to me.

"No need for the lies Aiden, I really don't care enough to be bothered. Vodka and coke when you're ready," I say; chucking some money on the bar.

We spend another hour chatting and dancing. Aria whispers to JP and he hauls her into his arms and over his shoulder. She screams with laughter.

"See you tomorrow Bella," she waves as he carries her from the club.

"Lucky bitch." sighs Jack. He gets up, "I'd better get back to Beck,"-he hugs me- "Call me if you need me."

Aiden stalks past me and heads to his office. He hasn't even looked in my direction since I played the recording. How dare he act like I'm the one in the wrong, when he lied.

I leave it ten minutes before I follow him and head up

to the apartment.

He's in the kitchen, topless. I notice the deep scratches across his back and nail marks on his shoulders. I roll my eyes at the fakeness of it all. I might not have had sex, but I've never known anyone to come away looking like they have wrestled with a tiger. She clearly marked him for my benefit.

"Laurie miss called you last night, she made sure you heard that stuff." he says turning to face me. I laugh

"Did she make you say all that shit too? Cos' that's what hurt me Aiden."

He nods, "I don't want your rent, friends help each other, I shouldn't have said any of that. I've not got many female friends, as you have probably guessed," he says, sheepishly.

I head to my room, "I'm moving out, so you can cross me off that female friend list." I say slamming my door.

Aiden

Damn that girl, she isn't moving out. I pace the kitchen. I'm a dick. All these games, I should have just chatted her up and fucked her. Once the damn paper work is signed, I can cut her loose. Jake said two months and I've only managed a couple of weeks, damn it.
I wonder for the thousandth time if there's any way around the damn deal, but I know there isn't. I've had enough people look over it.

I can't have her leave and I can't put up with the way she has me in knots like this. Fuck the plan, it's about time she realized exactly who I am and why I can't be with her.

I storm towards her room and refuse to let sense talk me around. I shove the door open and she's standing in a white lace bra with matching knickers. I momentarily forget what I was marching in here for, she's stolen my breath.

"What the hell are you doing?" she demands putting her hands on her hips. I get into her space and point my finger in her face.

"You aren't leaving, you belong here with me and yes I have fucked up, I probably will over and over but you aren't leaving here so stop looking for excuses to leave." She takes a second to gather herself but then her eyes fill with rage.

"How dare you march in here telling me what I can and can't do? You don't own me!"

It's like she's waved a red rag to a bull and my hand is around her throat, not tight but enough to shut her up. My lips are on hers, pushing my tongue into her mouth. It's not a gentle kiss like before, I'm taking it and she lets me, gripping my shoulders.

Bella

I hold onto his broad shoulders to stop myself from collapsing. The kiss is rough and demanding and it sends shock waves through my body. He grips my neck with one hand and his other is gripping my hair, gently tugging my head back. He moves his mouth across my cheek and down my neck, nipping and licking as he goes. My eyes are closed tight and I'm panting.

His hands loosen the hold and begin to caress my shoulders, then along my arms. He rests his forehead against my shoulder and I realize just how tall he is because he's slightly bent at the knee.

He lifts his head and something in his eyes looks torn.

"I really like you, and I don't know how to handle it," he confesses. "But while I figure it out, you're staying here," and then he leaves slamming my door behind him.

I stand staring after him, in a stunned silence. Is it wrong that I am completely turned on by his dominance?

I'm dreaming of Aiden, when I feel myself being lifted. I slowly open my eyes and find him staring at me.

"I just want to try something, go to sleep," he

whispers. I'm not sure if it's still my dream so I snuggle into his chest, enjoying the realness of it.

I wake and stretch out, my presses against a hard, hot body and I sit up quickly. I'm in Aiden's bed and he is fast asleep looking gorgeous with his arm above his head, completely at peace.

Why did he bring me in here, and how did I not wake to take full advantage of this situation? Maybe he was sleep walking, or maybe I was.

I quietly lift the sheet and bring my legs over to the edge of the bed. His hand lashes out fast and grips my wrist making me squeal.

"Where are you going?" His eyes remain closed.

"Why am I in here?" I'm only in a t-shirt, with no underwear. I wrestle with the bottom of the shirt, willing it to be longer.

"I needed to see what it feels like to sleep in the same bed," he mumbles the words, sleepily.

"You don't think that's something you should have cleared with me first?"

He opens one eye. "Lay down Bella, I don't do

talking first thing." He yanks me back into bed. I half fall on him and he wraps his arm around my waist, pulling my back to his front. I'm conscious of the fact that my t-shirt is riding up slightly and I do my best to pull it down again.

"Leave it. I'm not going to touch you." He shifts slightly, and I feel his hardness press against my bare ass. Thank god he's wearing bottoms. I am blushing with embarrassment but try to lay still. There's no way I can fall back to sleep now.

"You're thinking too much, it's keeping me awake," he mumbles into my hair.

"You can't hear me thinking," I sigh with a smile. He presses himself against me with a slight thrust and I take in a deep breath,

"Don't sass me, smart mouth."

We lay for some time before he releases his grip on me and rolls onto his back.

"I've got to head out to some meetings early today, I will drop you at work," he says, stretching. I watch his muscles bunch in protest.

"It's fine, I can take the tube," I sit up.

"It's not a request Bella. Go and shower in my bathroom." He nods to his on suite. He is being ridiculous, and this bossiness is going a bit far.

I stand and head straight to my own bathroom. I squeal as he lifts me from behind and carries me back to his bedroom. He puts me down in his bathroom and takes the hem of my t-shirt. I grip it and swat at his hands but with no effort at all he lifts it over my head and I'm standing naked in front of him.

I try to cover myself and give him my best death stare. He turns the shower on, ignoring my embarrassment completely. I notice my shower gel and toothbrush are in his bathroom. He shoves me towards the steaming shower and pushes me under the jets of hot water. I close my eyes and let the water wash over me.

The screen opens, and I'm gob smacked when Aiden steps into the shower, completely naked, his cock standing proudly in front of him. I try not to look, and I know my face is burning with embarrassment.

He gets my shower gel and squeezes some into his

hand, he rubs his hands to work it into a lather and I stand there watching his every move, dazed, in silence.

He turns me away from him and begins to run his hands over my shoulders and back. I close my eyes as he works the lather across my body avoiding my breasts and between my legs. I'm not sure if that disappoints me.

He takes my hand and squirts some of his shower gel into my hands. He turns his back to me and waits. He obviously wants me to wash him and I'm freaking out.

It's not like I've never touched a man before. Of course, I've done stuff with men, just not sex, but Aiden is hot and he's really big and I don't just mean his muscles. Am I supposed to stick to safe areas?

I begin to run my hands over his broad back. Ignoring the scratches, I take this time to study the art work across his torso. He turns, bringing my attention back to him. He places my hands on his chest and keeps hold of them, moving them slowly in circles, never letting his eyes leave mine.

He moves them further down, across his stomach until I brush his cock. He places my hand there and releases my wrist. I feel like he's testing me in some way, to see if I will run but I don't. Instead I grip his impressive shaft, enjoying the slight intake of breath he takes when I move my hand. I work my hand back and forth and he keeps his eyes on mine, staring into his eyes makes it feel so much more of a turn on. There's something about the power he's just handed me that has me panting as I work him.

He's close, I can tell by the hitch in his breath. He grips my shoulders and throws his head back on a roar as jets of his arousal leave his shaking body.

I've never watched a man that closely before. My embarrassment has long gone, instead I'm so turned on I'm pressing my thighs together to get some kind of friction.

"Fuck," he pants, bringing his eyes back to mine. He places his hand to my cheek and guides me towards him, gently kissing my lips. "You're going to make me late." He smiles against my lips.

I deepen the kiss and feel his cock slowly rising again.

Seriously, that can't be normal. I step back and rinse off under the shower. He lets me leave and begins rinsing himself off.

I get ready for work and meet him in the kitchen. He hands me a coffee in a travel mug and I follow him out to his car. It all feels so normal being with him, people passing would assume we were married, and this was our morning routine.

CHAPTER ELEVEN

Aiden

I can't concentrate on my first meeting. All I can think about is Bella and the way her tiny hands felt on me this morning. I didn't plan any of that, but the beast has taken over and I'm no longer listening to my sensible side. I'm going to find it hard to let her go when this is all over, but I can't keep her, she deserves better. Plus, she will hate me when she finds out about Jake and his stupid challenge. At least I feel like I'm back in control again and that makes me happy.

I head out to the car. JP starts the engine as I climb in. "You have a glint in your eye today boss, what're you up to?"

I smile and pull out my phone. I dial the local florist and order a hundred pounds worth of roses to be delivered to the bakery.

"I took Raff's advice, I took control and she likes it," I grin. JP looks horrified.

"You haven't fucked her though?" he asks.

I shake my head, "No, I can't do that until the end, it

will hurt less that way."

"I'm not convinced Aiden, this is going to break her regardless," he sighs. I know he's right but what choice have I got?

"Has Raff sorted the end game, like, how is this going to play out?" he asks.

"The doctors already sorted, Jake did that. I'm going to convince her to go for a check-up after the deed. Raff's right, I can't do any of this unless she falls for me in some way because why would she do any of the shit I need her do afterwards, unless she's blinded by love?" JP nods in agreement and I know he's back on my side.

"How was your night with Aria?" I grin changing the subject.

"Wild! I've never met anyone like her, we have this crazy night, she showed me moves that I've never seen before, and you know how many tricks I've learned along the way. Then she practically kicks me out this morning man. I'm so confused."

I look at him with an astonished expression.

"What?" he asks.

"You sound like a girl," I say. "Replay in your head what you have just said out loud and you will want to cut your tongue out," I laugh.

He shrugs as he pulls the truck into the car park for our next meeting.

"I feel like she's grabbed me by the balls and tattooed her name all over them. I can't stop thinking about her," he whines. I slap him upside the head.

"Pull yourself together, will yah? A month and a half left, and we can tag team a whole bunch of girls at the click of my fingers. Now get a grip."

Bella

It's been two weeks since our moment in the shower. He hasn't touched me like that since and it's killing me.

I'm trying to play it cool but I'm slowly losing my mind. He insists that I share his bed every night and despite the fact that every night when I go to sleep and every morning when I wake up, his cock is poking my back, he hasn't touched me in that way. He's given me lots of mind-blowing kisses and he's the best at cuddles but I'm starting to wonder if he doesn't see me in that way.

Aria thinks I'm crazy and that Aiden is being a gentlemen and that he is waiting for me to show him I'm ready. I disagree. Aiden is so domineering that I know he doesn't want me to make the move.

I'm getting ready to spend the night in the VIP area at Tremos. It's becoming a regular weekend hangout for me and Aria. She hooked JP in and is now playing a game where she completely ignores him. I admire her confidence because it's actually working. JP is like a love-sick puppy dog begging for her attention. She said the sex was amazing, so I couldn't understand why she risked pushing him away, but it's paying off.

I spray my dark curls and give them a little shake. I want to look perfect tonight to see if I can tempt Aiden to at least touch me. Aria hands me her red lipstick and I apply it.

"I've invited a few of the girls," she informs me as we make our way down in the lift. It opens into Aiden's office and he's on the phone. His eyes bug out of his head when he takes in the short red dress I'm wearing. It clings to every curve and stops just below my ass cheeks. I definitely can't bend over in this dress.

I give him a smile and a little wave as we pass through, I'm almost through the door when I hear his heavy foot steps behind me. He halts me, gripping my hair and gently pulling me back into his office, leaving Aria on the other side of the door, he slams it shut and flicks the lock.

"What the fuck are you wearing Isabella?" he grates out in my ear; I shiver and smile.

"Do you like it? Its new."

"No, I don't like it, your ass is hanging out of it," he snaps, turning me to face him, his hand still gripping my hair. I press my hands to his chest and lean towards him, when he sees my intention, he loosens his grip. I gently kiss along his jaw line and when I reach his mouth I lick along his lower lip until he opens for me. I gently kiss him, dipping my tongue in and out of his mouth teasing him. I let out a slight moan because I know he likes that.

I feel his cock press against my stomach and I smile, rubbing against him.

"What game are you playing Bells?" he asks cocking his eyebrow suspiciously.

"I dressed for you," I whisper. He smirks and pulls harder on my hair.

"Are you seducing me Isabella?" I nod. He unfastens his button and lets his trousers drop to the floor, he pushes me to my knees. "Kneel!" he says firmly, and I do.

He keeps hold of my hair and uses his other hand to push his boxers down.

"Put your hands behind your back," he orders. He

guides his hard shaft towards my mouth and I lick the end causing him to suck in a breath. I press my tongue to the base and firmly run it along the bottom until I reach the tip, and then I wrap my mouth around him sucking him in as far as I can without my gag reflex kicking in.

He grips my hair tight, stilling my mouth and mutters a string of curses. He guides my head back and forth, picking up the pace as he fucks my mouth.

There's a knock on the door and I still, but he takes my hair and forces me to keep moving.

"Fuckoff!"

"I need the keys to the stock room," says Raff through the door.

"Tough shit, fuck off."

He lets go of me and grips the desk. I know he's close and I can hear Raff outside bitching to someone about not being able to get the keys.

I grip the base of his cock and he slaps my hand away.

"Did I say you could move your hands?" he pants, and I place them behind my back.

Aiden

There's something sexy about a gorgeous woman on her knees, hands behind her back, sucking your cock and looking up at you like she wants you to fuck her in any way you'd like. The sight of Bella, in her short red dress, doing that exact thing has me weak in the knees.

I can hear Raff moaning outside about needing to get shit done, so I pick up my pace and she takes it all. I don't like to think about how she became this good at sucking cock.

I grip the desk again.

"Look at me," I grit out. As soon as her eyes meet mine, I let go and release into her mouth. She swallows every drop like I'm the best thing she's ever tasted, and it takes everything in me not to haul her over my desk and fuck her until she screams.

I pull her to her feet and kiss her forehead.

"Go and change, you can't wear that out there." I dismiss her, heading to the door while fastening my button. Raff looks pissed off and I smile.

"Chill out Raff, come in, get the keys," I say, opening

the door wider so he can enter. Bella still stood there looking annoyed.

"Didn't you hear me?" I ask her.

"Yes, I heard, but I'm not getting changed, I love this dress," she says defiantly and heads out of the door.

Raff laughs. "That told you!"

I find her at the bar, leaning over slightly so that the bartender can hear her. The dress has ridden up and is showing the bottom of her ass cheeks and I see red. I stand behind her and she looks over her shoulder.

"Hey," she grins wiggling her perfect round ass against me.

"I'm giving you one chance to go and change," I say. She laughs and turns to face me, amusement in her eyes.

"Stop being a freak Aiden, I wore the dress for you, you're being ungrateful."

I take a deep breath, she's pushing me. I bend forward and place my shoulder to her stomach, hauling her over my shoulder. She screams and hits my back.

"Aiden put me down!" she screeches. I slap her ass hard and march back to my office. I press for the lift, all the while she hits my back, screaming and yelling. I slap her ass again and she quietens down.

We get back into the apartment and I go straight to the bedroom. I throw her on the bed and rip the walk-in wardrobe doors open. I rummage for a minute and she watches me in amusement. I reappear with a black jumpsuit and throw it at her. She sighs and stands up.

"You're being ridiculous."

I fold my arms and lean against the door.

"You aren't leaving this apartment until you're half decent," I say firmly. She grins, and I watch as she lifts her barely there dress up, and over her head.

"No fucking underwear?" I yell.

She laughs. "I can't wear underwear with that dress, it's too tight!"

She is trying to kill me, I groan. I am glad I didn't know this little snippet of information before I had her on her knees, or I definitely would have bent her over my desk.

I head back to the wardrobe and dig out some underwear. I throw it onto the bed. "Don't even think about putting that on until you have knickers on," I huff, and she rolls her eyes.

CHAPTER TWELVE

Bella

"It worked," I grin, handing Aria her drink. She looks annoyed and I follow her glare over to JP who has a girl sitting on his knee, laughing. "Oh dear, what happened to the game?" I ask, sitting down. She throws her drink back.

"He's not playing it right," she says. I laugh, and she glares at me.

"How can he play when he doesn't know the rules Ari? You've ignored him for ages. Just be straight with him," I say.

"He is a man, they are the masters of games Bella, trust me, he's just playing by his own rules. I will win him back though," she says confidently, "So, he fell for the dress?"

"He didn't exactly touch me, but I got to touch him again." I shrug. She looks confused.

"So far he's had all the fun then!" she states.

"I enjoy pleasing him," I say defensively. She shakes her head in disgust.

"Honestly Bella, you need to listen to yourself, you aren't here to please him! You want to give him your cherry, you had better stop giving him all the pleasure. You need to hold out until he's fit to burst," she advises.

I glance over at JP who has his tongue stuck down the girl's throat and shake my head.

"I'm not listening to you if that's how it's going to end up!"

She scowls at me and I laugh.

Later, Raff and Aiden join us at our booth. I'm feeling the vodka rushing through my veins.

Aiden moves the bottle out of my reach. It's a subtle move but one I notice, and it annoys me. I reach for it, but he intercepts my reach, pulling my hand into his.

"Aiden," I pull my hand away, "I want a drink." He shakes his head and signals for the waitress to come over. She smiles at him shyly as he hands her the bottle.

"Please remove this before I have to carry her home," he smiles.

She takes it, her fingers gently brushing his.

"What was that?" I say, glaring between them.

I know my brain isn't thinking rationally at the moment but I'm very annoyed that he took it upon himself to cut my drinking off and then proceeded to humiliate me in front of his new bartender. He gives her a smile and she heads back to the bar.

"I'm not an alcoholic, you totally made me out to be one just then!" He pulls me into his side and when I try to pull away, he slides his hand into my hair. Subtly he grips it and angles my head towards his mouth.

"Stop!" he growls, and I do instantly.

There's a command in his voice that sends shivers straight to my knickers.

"Aiden, why haven't you slept with her yet?" slurs Aria and I kick her under the table.

"I sleep with her every night," he says, sipping his drink and looking around the crowded bar casually.

"But you haven't fucked her yet," she carries on, ignoring my glares.

I grab Aiden's arm and stand. "I think we should go," I say.

He places his hand over mine and stills me.

"Is that what you want Bella?" he asks, amusement in his voice and I cringe. Aria and her stupid drunken mouth.

"No, ignore her, she thinks everyone wants sex. She's just pissed off because JP isn't playing her stupid game," I blurt.

Aiden places his hands on my face and brings my lips to his.

I hear Aria sigh. "I wish someone would kiss me like that."

"Stop playing games then," grumbles JP.

"I'm not going to touch you until you ask me to Bella," whispers Aiden, placing little kisses along my mouth.

I want to blurt out that he can touch me now, but I know my sober brain will only hate my drunken brain tomorrow, so I just smile.

The next morning, I wake up to find the usual prodding in my back. I sense that Aiden is awake, his breathing is fast and he's moving against me. I remember what Aria said last night, about holding out more so I sit up, moving away from him. He frowns but doesn't say anything.

"I need coffee," I groan, getting up. He watches me, and I see his hand moving up and down his shaft. He has no shame and doesn't try to hide the fact that he's masturbating in front of me.

I resist the urge to help him out and head to the kitchen, chanting over and over in my head, *I can do this.*

I power up Aiden's laptop and sit at the kitchen table sipping my coffee. I need to look for a flat. I know Aiden doesn't want me to, but I've heard nothing from Dad's little dealings, so I assume it's all blown over. If me and Aiden are going places, then I don't want to be under his feet. He hasn't said that we are an item, I know he doesn't have girlfriends and he insists that he can't have relationships but if he did it once then surely, he can do it again.

Aria thinks that if I try to put a label on it, I will scare him away.

I'm in his bed, I don't think he sees any other women, he's always around me, so I'm pretty certain we are an item. I smile to myself.

The screen lights up and there's a picture of Aiden with his arm around another guy. They are both smiling at the camera and I see similarities in their appearance.

"What are you doing Bella?" I jump at Aiden's stern voice. He pulls the laptop away and closes the lid.

"I know that guy," I say, confused "He used to come in the shop all the time."
Aiden closes his eyes for a moment like he's arguing with himself.

"Jake," he mutters. "My brother."

Aiden

Great. What are the rules if she discovers Jake even though I didn't tell her?

"I used to look forward to him coming in every week," she smiles and then it fades. "When he stopped coming in, I thought he had moved away or finally met someone."

"Well now yah know, he died!" I inwardly flinch at my bluntness. "Why were you on my laptop anyway?"

"We shared stories every week of our dating nightmares," she continues, I can see the heart break in her eyes and I feel like a bastard for dismissing her. "He wouldn't tell me his name, I would ask every time and it became more like a game."

Part of me doesn't want to know why Jake chose her, it would make it even more personal now that I've gotten to know her.

This is already one huge mess and I feel it's about to get worse.

I make her another coffee and sit opposite her.

"He was a fuck up at dating," I say.

A tear rolls down her cheek and she gives me a sad smile.

"We would play top trumps on the worst dates," she laughs, brushing her tears away, "Every week I'd ask his name and each time he would say 'not yet Bella, it's more fun like this.' He wouldn't tell me anything about his life other than his dating stories."

Sounds just like something Jake would do. He liked to flirt and reel them in, play games, just like now.

I pull her to stand and wrap her in my arms. I kiss her head and hold her tight. She clings to me and it feels good to hold her.

"I want you to be my first," she whispers, and my grip tightens.

"Bella, you're upset." I don't know why I'm trying to talk her out of it, when this is what I've been waiting for. It feels wrong, taking something so special from her when she doesn't know the truth.

"I want to Aiden, I've waited so long to feel this spark, I don't want to wait anymore," she smiles reaching up to kiss me. I pull back and she looks at me with hurt in her eyes.

"Don't you want me?" she asks, quietly.

I make a decision, I need to pacify her until I work out what the hell is going on in my head. I lift her onto the table and stand between her legs. I run my hands down her face and hold her still, taking my time to kiss her slow. She relaxes into me and I lift her arms. I pull my t-shirt that she wears to bed over her head. She bites her bottom lip and leans back slightly, pushing her breasts forward.

I take her nipple in my mouth and suck, keeping my eyes on her face as I swirl my tongue over the bud that's now puckered in my mouth. She hisses when I nip it, releasing it and giving the same attention to her other breast.

I pull her hands out in front of her and take the discarded t-shirt. I wrap it around her wrists and expertly tie it. Pulling it tight enough to mark her golden skin. I press her shoulders indicating that I want her to lay down, she does so, and I place her hands above her head.

I watch her skin break out into goose bumps as I run

my finger down her stomach. I avoid the area where she wants me the most and I trail my finger along her thigh. She presses her legs together to suppress the ache and I gently part her legs. She goes to cover herself with her bound hands, but I stop her and push them back above her head.

I begin the slow trail again and she groans in frustration. I place my hands on each of her thighs and push them apart, wide. I see she's wet and my cock feels like it's going to explode in my pants. She's squirming, and I press her hips to the table to hold her still.

I can smell her arousal and its driving me wild. I bend so my face is close, she can feel my breath there and she squirms some more, trying to get my face where she needs it.

I run my tongue straight up her wetness and she cries out. She goes to move her hands but remembers my instruction and places them back above her head. I smile, she is begging to be dominated.

I explore her with my tongue, she's moaning and panting, when I think she can't take much more I circle her clit with my thumb and she yells my name, her body shakes, and I revel in the fact that she's orgasmed so hard, there are tears running down her face. I stand and lick my thumb. She gives me a lazy smile.

"My bones have turned to mush," she whispers. I stand between her legs and guide them to wrap around my hips. I pull her to sitting position and place her bound arms over my head. I lift her, pressing my hard cock against her clit and she shakes involuntary. She presses her face into my neck and I head for the bedroom. I want to spend my Saturday worshipping her body, seeing how many times I can make her come without using my cock.

CHAPTER THIRTEEN

Bella

It's not possible, I can't orgasm anymore. I'm breathless, I'm sweating, and rolling around gripping his head between my legs. He hasn't given me a break since my last orgasm not five minutes ago.

He won't penetrate me, not even with his finger, despite my begging. Not that I'm complaining, because I feel like I'm flying right now. I'm not sure where I start, and he ends. He holds me still and a scream rips through my lungs as I shudder. I roll away from him, "No more," I groan. "I can't take anymore."

He swats my ass and sits up.

"Remember what happened last time you said that," he grins.

We have spent the entire day in bed. We have explored each other over and over. The man is a machine.

We lay facing each other and he runs his hand up and down my ribs. I decide that I need the label, I know Aria would be screaming at me to shut the fuck up right now, but I need something.

167

"Where is this going?" I ask quietly. He thinks for a minute.

"Depends what you mean."

"Us," I push and I see a flicker of panic in his eyes.

"Bella, we have talked about this," he sighs, his hand stills on my ribs. "I don't do the happily ever after shit." I nod, hiding my disappointment. "We are having fun, aren't we?" I nod again. "Look I like you, you know I do and right now I'm enjoying this," he explains, pointing back and forth between us. "But if you want me to give you an official girlfriend title, I'm sorry, I can't."

He sits up and swings his legs over the edge of the bed. His back is to me. I regret asking, I've broken the spell we were under just moments ago. I could kick myself.

"For the record, I'm glad I'm not your girlfriend," I say to lighten the mood. He glances over his shoulder with a smirk.

"Yeah?" he grins.

I nod, "I am free to explore what orgasms feel like from normal human men." I grin, and he spins around fast, diving on top of me and pinning my arms above my head.

"Normal human men?" he queries, and I nod innocently.

"Men that aren't robots with a constant hard on." I laugh, and he kisses me hard.

"You can look, but you will be sorely disappointed in what you find young Isabella," he says in his best Drogo accent. I giggle as he moves down my body, licking my nipple.

"It's unfair to keep my virgin body to yourself," I groan, and he lifts his head slightly to meet my gaze.

"I haven't finished with it yet," he grins.

I decide to stay in Saturday night. I've had so many late nights that my body is refusing to move from the couch. Aria is coming over later to watch films, which works out well because I will be on my own, Aiden is at the club tonight.

I admire him in his expensive suit as he fastens the cuff links. His handsome chiseled jaw, his bright blue eyes and the way his hair lays perfectly to one side makes my insides melt. I feel like the luckiest girl alive right now and I know that he's going to be my first.

"What are you smiling about?" he asks, checking his hair in the mirror by the door.

"Just thinking how lucky I am."

He pauses, mid hair sort, and eyes me through the mirror.

"Just remember what I said earlier Bella, this isn't a relationship."

I wince, recovering quick, "Jesus Aiden, stop putting yourself on that pedestal," I snap. "I get the message, alright?" He approaches me and bends, gently kissing my head.

"Right, okay, well I'll maybe see you later then," he shrugs and leaves.

Maybe see me later, what the hell does that mean? I'm scowling as I glare at the closed door.

Aria is late, she is always either far too early or late. I sigh and finish my coffee. I've spent the last hour sketching some new wedding cake designs for us to add to our shop portfolio.

I finally hear the bell from the elevator, announcing her arrival. I unlatch the door so she can come straight in.

There's a bang and a yell. I rush to the door and poke my head out to see Aria and JP. He is glaring at her and I notice she's only wearing one shoe.

"Hey, what's going on?" I ask, quietly, scared that if I speak too loudly, they may start yelling.

"Your friend is fucking crazy," states JP holding up Aria's shoe. "Missed my head by an inch!"

"I hate you!" she shouts. "Stop following me, I don't want to hear any more bull shit excuses!"

The elevator pings again and Aiden storms out looking furious. "What the fuck was that?" he aims at Aria. I fold my arms across my chest when Laurie appears behind him.

She looks amazing and it makes me want to scratch her eyes out. I also want to run back inside and hide seeing as I am wearing one of Aiden's t-shirts that just about covers my butt and my hair is piled up on my head.

She places a well-manicured hand gently on his arm, "Calm down Aide," she soothes, and I see the way he takes a deep breath as if to calm himself.

"Aria, my VIP area is a mess, what the hell are you playing at?" he asks more calmly, and Laurie rubs his arm as if to praise him. I roll my eyes in annoyance.

"Ask your dumb ass friend!" snaps Aria. "Who can't keep it in his pants for more than an hour."

Aiden turns to JP. "I warned you this would happen," he growls and JP shrugs.

"The girl is a nut job, just bar her and get her out of my sight," he snaps.

Aria lets out a scream and throws a vase of plastic flowers from the table near the front door. It smashes into tiny pieces against the wall behind JP's head.

"Fuck Aria, sort your shit out you crazy bitch!" yells JP

"You complete bastard!" she squeaks out and then she begins to cry. I venture out into the hall and pull her into a hug.

"She needs to go," orders Aiden, "NOW!" he adds glaring at me.

"I agree, look at the mess she's made," says Laurie.

"I've told you before to stop inviting waifs and strays into your home Aiden."

I sigh and rub Aria's back. "She's my friend Aiden, I'm not kicking her out. JP has clearly upset her."

"Well you know where the door is!" snaps Laurie.

"I will be putting you through the damn door if you speak to me again," I warn.

She puts her hand in Aiden's. "Are you going to let your bit on the side speak to me in that way?" she asks.

He doesn't move her hand away, he lets her hold it and my blood boils. I take a deep breath and remind myself that he isn't mine, he can be with whoever he likes.

"Isabella it's not up for discussion, she has trashed my booth in the VIP area, she has smashed a vase against my apartment wall. I can't let that slide," he says firmly.

"She has ruined my Saint Laurent bag," adds Laurie. "It has sentimental value, it's the one you got me for our first Christmas."

He has the decency to look uncomfortable, he clearly sees what we all see, that she wants to mark her territory.

I decide to show her that it isn't me forcing my way into Aiden's life, it's him that insists I stay. It's about time the spineless bastard shows her just how forceful he can be. Although I am pretty sure she has seen this side many times, usually when she's naked, I huff at the thought bringing everyone's eyes to me.

"You're right Aiden," I smile sweetly, Aria lifts her head to look at me.

"Huh?" she asks. I pull her back into a hug, just to hide the state of her running mascara and crazy hair.

"Can she just wait while I get my stuff together?" I ask innocently, and I see the panic cross his eyes. I lead Aria back into the apartment.

"What are you doing?" she hisses, and I smile one of my *'trust me'* smiles.

He marches in behind me, Laurie hot on his heels.

"What are you talking about?" he demands, and I turn to face him.

"I'm going to move in to Aria's until I find a flat. I've got a few viewings lined up for next week already so it's not a problem." I see his face turn red with anger and

Laurie tries the old rubbing of the arm trick. I raise an eyebrow, he notices, and moves away slightly.

Laurie scowls. "I think that's for the best actually Aiden. I can come here then instead of us sneaking around in hotels."

"You wouldn't have to sneak around at all if you just left your husband!" I suggest with a smile.

"You wouldn't even be here if he didn't want your virginity so badly," she counters, and I laugh.

"And how does that feel? To know I have something you gave away long ago?"

Aiden puts up his hands, "ENOUGH!" he yells, "Bella, you aren't going anywhere. Aria I'm billing you for the damages and I don't want to see you drinking in my club for at least a month."

Aiden

I am so angry I want to put my fist through the wall. Stupid JP and all his drama. I have had enough of him bringing shit to my door, but I will save that argument for another time.

Right now, I'm waiting to see if Bella is going to try and leave. I say *try* because there's no way I'm letting her walk. How the fuck did JP's argument with Aria end up being mine and Bella's argument?

Laurie seems to be everywhere I turn at the moment. Coming to the club, hanging around my booth, touching me at every damn opportunity she gets.

I'm keeping her around for the minute because I need Bella to see that I'm not the settling down type of guy. If Laurie is still on the scene then Bella won't keep getting these stupid ideas that we are going to fall in love and be something we are never going to be, a couple.

I've got two more weeks and then it will be over with. Raff came up with a better plan, not involving doctors or examinations. If it all works and the timing is spot on, it should all work out nicely.

Laurie stands in front of me and places her hands on my chest.

"It makes more sense if she just goes to stay at her friend's. Look at the trouble it's causing just having her here. You say there's nothing between you, so just let her leave," she says quietly.

"I've seen and heard enough Aiden, I won't stay here while she's around you, so I'm leaving," says Bella. heading for our bedroom. I follow her, and Laurie follows me.

I silently say a prayer to the good lord than no harm comes to my apartment now that JP and Aria are alone.

"She's sleeping in your bedroom?" snaps Laurie, shoving me. I don't budge, I'm triple her size. Bella drags her case from under my bed. I could let her go, I could just get her to meet me that specific night and seduce her, but if it fails then I won't get another try. If I keep her here and keep her under my spell, then there's more chance of it working out the way I want it to. Plus, while she's here, she isn't dating anyone else and she won't get any stupid ideas of sleeping with anyone else.

"I don't need an audience," says Bella, heading for the built-in wardrobe. I move the case and place it back under the bed.

"Laurie is my friend Bella," I try to reason.

She places a pile of clothes on the bed and reaches under to pull the case back out, dumping it next to the clothes.

"I know. This is about Aria," she nods, unzipping the case and flinging it open. "But three is a crowd and if I'm honest, I'm not comfortable knowing that you are sleeping with her then coming back to me and…" she stops talking, realizing that she doesn't want to say what we do out loud and I grin, annoying her more.

"Oh god, tell me you aren't messing around with this girl," groans Laurie. "Why would you?"

"For heaven sake, haven't you got a husband to annoy?" Bella says, throwing her clothes into the case and going back into the wardrobe. I begin removing stuff from her case.

"You aren't going anywhere," I say again, and she appears, shifting me out of her way with her hip.

"Let her go Aiden, I'm free tonight, I can spend the night," purrs Laurie. Bella stops and sighs.

"You say you don't want a relationship, you tell me you can't commit but you won't let me leave. Aiden, I don't want to give you me, if you can't even give us a try."

"How the hell did we get to this!" I shout, throwing my hands up in frustration. "I just wanted Aria to go and now you want to go unless I make us official?"

"I sleep in your bed, not by choice but because you carry me in here if I even try to go into my own room. I can't bathe or shower unless you're in there with me. You tie me up and do amazing things to my body, you take me and pick me up from work," she says counting on her fingers. "What do you think that is Aiden? You're doing all of the things that boyfriends do."

"Except sleep with you," cuts in Laurie. "He hasn't had sex with you, but he comes to me for that, so I guess he's just keeping you around for company. How boring!"

Bella lets out a scream and charges for Laurie, I managed to grab her around the waist before she reaches her, and I hold her against me.

"Laurie go and wait out there," I order.

"Get her out of this apartment right now or I will rip her cheap extensions out!" yells Bella, in warning. I sigh and nod at Laurie who looks outraged.

"Babe just go, I will call you later when I've sorted this," I say.

"If you don't show tonight Aiden, that's done. I'm sick of this drama. I don't make excuses for you to let me down," she warns and storms out.

"What's going on Bella?" I ask turning her to face me. "You were cool with all this earlier, I explained the situation."

She shrugs, "I hate seeing you with her."

"We have a past Bella, I can't help that."

"I know, I'm being unreasonable. I shouldn't make any demands on you, but it's not fair. If we aren't together and you don't want to commit, then I should be able to see whoever I want. I should be able to meet other men and that shouldn't bother you!"

It does bother me, it bothers me a lot. The thought of

her with another man, letting him kiss her or touch her makes my blood boil.

"It bothers me," I admit. "But not because I'm in love with you Bella, it's because I'm selfish and controlling. I want you all to myself and I want you to only have me on your mind." She shakes her head in disgust and resumes packing.

"You're a bastard."

I still her hands and pull her towards me.

"I haven't pretended I'm not. I was a bastard last night when you let me do all of those things to you. I was still a bastard today when you were sucking my cock and I will still be a bastard tonight when I go and fuck Laurie."

She pulls away from me, tears forming in her eyes.

"Do not touch me again, don't even come near me," she chokes out.

"Until later when you're in my bed," I say. "Because let's face it, you aren't going anywhere, you have nowhere to go and you thought that by putting me in that position with Laurie you would be able to force my hand, but its back fired because I can still go and fuck Laurie and then I can come back to you and you will snuggle up to me, let me do whatever I want and the cycle will continue. I didn't change the fucking rules Bella!" I yell. I walk out, leaving her to accept the fact that I am not boyfriend material.

JP has left, and Aria is on the sofa flicking through her phone.

"She might need you," I say, and she looks up. "She's upset," I add. Aria huffs and mutters something about men being bastards as she heads to the bedroom.

It's a big risk pushing her like that, but she needed to see the real me. I head down to the club and hope to god she doesn't leave.

CHAPTER FOURTEEN

Aria

I've never felt it before. I've read about it in stories but reading about it doesn't do it justice. Heartbreak, my first heartbreak. Aria hands me another tissue.

"So, are you leaving then?" I shrug, and her eyes go wide. "Bells, he's a complete bastard. Why would you even think about staying here?"

"He's right, he didn't make me promises of hearts and roses, he told me from the start there was nothing in it, that he couldn't be in a relationship. I could leave but I'm happier here even when he's a bastard," I admit.

She flops back onto the bed. "I don't get it, the more he pushes you away the tighter you cling. I mean, you're happy to let him sleep with anyone he wants to and then come here and drag you into his bed. It's not right."

"I know it's messed up, I can't explain it. It's like he's got this pull on me and I know I should just walk away but I feel this need to be here."

"Well you need to sleep in your own room Bella, you need to put some distance between you both because this has heart break written all over it."

I nod in agreement, "How did you leave it with JP?" She rolls her eyes.

"Yah know, I walked into the club and he was practically having sex with some bitch, grinding up her, but was texting me all last night telling me he really liked me and didn't want to play games! Fuck men, fuck JP. I am not being the play thing that waits around for him to decide if he wants me or not," she huffs, and I wince. It's exactly what I am doing with Aiden, and when Aria realizes what she's said, I see the panic in her face. "I'm so sorry Bella, I didn't mean you, I just meant..." she trails off.

"Don't worry about it."

After Aria leaves, I move my clothes and the rest of my stuff back into my room. I fit a bolt onto my bedroom door, I'd brought it when I first came but had never gotten around to doing it. I know that if I don't lock my door, he will carry me to his bed when he gets in and as much as I really want to be in his bed, I know I can't. He's been honest and now I have to back off because I can feel my heart falling for him.

I text my Dad. I've been checking in with him weekly and he seems to be doing okay. Now that I've been away from home, I feel the pressure has lifted. Because I'm not around to take care of the bills he seems to be taking on the responsibility. He tells me about a woman he's met, saying that they have been on a couple of dates. It would be nice to see my dad move on, he's been mourning my mum for far too long.

I add a bit of color to the cake designs I did earlier, anything to keep my mind off Aiden and what he's up to. I decide that I need to get to sleep and stop pining after a man that doesn't want me.

Aiden

I sit at my desk, my head in my hands. I am putting off going back to the apartment in case she's gone, and I've fucked it all up.

JP and Raff are sitting opposite me, feet up on my desk.

"Look if she's gone then she has, maybe this wasn't meant to be. We can get other clubs," says JP.

I shake my head, "If she goes then I will get her back, I'll have to lie and do the whole relationship thing until the paperwork is signed. I'm not losing it all, me and Jake worked hard to build this all up."

"Man, you can't do that, she doesn't deserve any of this. She's a nice girl and all this is going to fuck her up enough without making her promises you have no intention of keeping. This was all good on paper but now we know her, it doesn't sit right with me," sighs Raff.

"Don't you think I know all that Raff, but what choice do I have?" I yell, making him jump. "I don't deserve to lose all of this, I don't know what Jake was thinking but if he wasn't already dead, I would fucking kill him!"

It's almost five in the morning when I decide I can't hide any more. I open the bedroom door quietly and freeze, she isn't there. I march over to the wardrobe and fling open the door. All her stuff has gone. I check my bathroom and it's the same, empty. Shit this was not how it was supposed to go.

I head towards the spare room, just to make sure and when I try the door it doesn't budge. Surely, she wouldn't have put a lock on the door. I give it a shoulder barge and it doesn't budge. I gently knock.

"Bella are you in there?" I whisper. I hear rustling. "Bella," I say a little louder. She doesn't answer but I know she's in there, I can sense it. "BELLA!" I'm banging on the door. How dare she lock me out of my own spare room? I know she's done this so that I can't put her in my bed.

"Go away Aiden," she mumbles.

"Open the door Isabella," I demand, I'm annoyed but I can't help feeling relief that she didn't go.

"No," she huffs. "Go away. I'm trying to sleep."

I rest my forehead against the door. "Don't you want

me to keep you warm?"

"No, you made yourself perfectly clear earlier, I'm done being your toy!" she says, and I smile as I head to my room. That's what she thinks.

I hear banging followed by Bella's giggling. I check the time, It's nine in the morning. I sigh, three hours sleep is not enough but now I'm awake I'm intrigued to see if I can still reel her in. Call me sadistic.

I head for the lounge in just my boxers. Bella is bent over wearing tight leggings and a sporty crop top. A large man is helping her straighten her leg.

"What the fuck is going on?"

She looks at me through the one leg she still has planted on the floor and smiles.

"Morning Aiden, this is Cal. Cal this is my landlord."

I scowl at her. *Landlord!* What game is she playing now? Cal heads my way, his hand out and I shake it reluctantly.

"Good to meet you Aiden, I'm Bella's personal trainer."

Well, that's new.

"I didn't know you had a personal trainer."

She stands up and places her hands on her hips, drawing my attention to her flat stomach. She's showing far too much skin.

"You don't know anything about my life, I like to keep fit." I catch her checking out Cal's ass in his tight shorts and I raise my eyebrows. She wiggles hers when she sees I've caught her. "I've neglected my sessions since all the stuff with my Dad, I've decided to get back on it and Cal here is amazing at working my body hard, aren't you Cal?"

He smiles at her and I recognized that look. He wants to fuck her, and it makes me want to punch him.

Bella

After my work out with Cal I can hardly walk. I'm lying on the grass in the park feeling like my lungs are about to burst and Cal is rubbing my leg muscles. I won't lie, it feels good. Which makes me wonder if there are other men that could make me feel as amazing as Aiden does with just one touch.

Cal has asked me out so many times I've lost count. He's good looking in an Essex boy kind of way, Muscles, tan and white teeth. Maybe I just need to bite the bullet.

"Yah know, my flat is just over there," nods Cal as if reading my mind. "We could cool down and then have a coffee? Look at sorting out a proper food plan?" I put my hand out for him to pull me up.

"Lead the way."

I'm looking over Cal's shoulder at the laptop he is typing away on. He's got me agreeing to extra sessions and he's drawn up a healthy eating plan.

I pull my phone out and send off a text to Aria.

I think I'm going to jump Cal! I've just clicked send, when it beeps in my hand.

What???? is her response. I smile and reply.

He's fit, he actually likes me, and I need to get over Aiden. You always tell me that to get over someone you get under someone else!!! I put the phone back in my bra top and take a deep breath, here goes.

I brush my finger across his cheek, and he turns slightly smiling, before I can back out, I move towards him making my intentions very clear. He doesn't move away, so I take that as a green light and I gently kiss his lips. His hands go to my face. He stands slowly, kissing me gently.

It's not like Aiden's kiss, there's no urgency or roughness in it, but I like it.

He turns us so that I'm against the table and I run my hands across his broad shoulders. I let his hands roam across the bare skin on my stomach and then slowly they run up my arms until they get to the straps of my bra top. He slowly pulls them down exposing my breasts. He kisses along my collar bone and I grip a hand into his hair as he makes his way down to my breasts. As I place my phone on the table, I see it flashing with Aiden's name. I put it face down.

Cal's fingers hook into my leggings and he peels them down my legs. He kneels in front of me and gently guides my leg over his shoulder. I feel his mouth on my opening and grip the table throwing my head back.

He takes his time tasting me. His licks are slow and intentional, even when I'm screaming his name, he keeps the same pace, it drives me wild.

"Let go Bella," he growls, and I shake my way through an intense orgasm. He stands and lowers his shorts, kissing me. I can taste myself on his lips.

"You sure about this?" he asks, I nod. He reaches over to a drawer and opens it. After fiddling around in there for a second, he pulls out a condom and rips it open. I watch him pull it over his hard erection.

I'm debating whether I should tell him that I'm a virgin, does it make a difference?

There's a bang at the door. We both look at each other and freeze like we're doing something wrong.

"BELLA, BELLA, open up!" It takes me a second to process that it's Aiden at the door.

"Shit, is it locked?" I whisper in a panic.

"I thought you said you were single?" asks Cal confused. We are standing looking at each other in silence. I can't work out if he's still outside or gone.

"Bells, please, please don't do it. I'll do whatever you want but please don't have sex with him," he begs.

Cal steps away from me and pulls his shorts up.

"You want to go and sort that?" he asks. I pull my clothes on and head for the door. I pull the safety chain on because Aiden can be unpredictable, and I don't want Cal to get hurt because of me. I peek out.

"What are you doing here Aiden? How did you even find me?" I whisper hiss. I take satisfaction in the fact that he looks desperate and ruffled, like he's in pain.

"Have you done it? Did you sleep with him?" he asks.

My phone lights up and Aria is calling me. I answer. She sounds panicked.

"Bella, Aiden is heading over. I am so sorry. JP saw the message and rang him. He completely freaked, I had to tell him where Cal lives," she rushes out.

"It's okay Ari, he's here," I say and hang up.

"I'm sorry, I've been a dick. I like you, I will do it, for you. I will try the relationship thing. I need you in my life, so please tell me I'm not too late?"

I can't speak, the words won't come. It's what I want but he was so adamant that he couldn't be in a relationship, there has to be more to all of this.

"You're not too late," I mutter. He lets out a huge breath of relief and smiles.

"Thank god, open the door Bells."

"I almost did though, you literally knocked as he was putting a condom on." I need to see if he's genuine and part of me needs to hurt him like he did me last night, with his harsh words.

Anger floods his face and his fists ball.

"Open the door!" he grits out.

"I wanted to see if it was different from you and me," I continue.

"Open the door!"

"He's not rough like you, he takes his time like he wants to be with me."

"I want to be with you Bella," Aiden reassures me.

"I'm ready to try, just open the door, you need to be in my arms."

"Would you still feel the same knowing I had his head between my legs just minutes ago?" I push. He shakes his head like he is trying to block out the image. "He made me cum in his mouth!"

"I know you want to hurt me Bella/ God knows I've done it to you enough, so yeah, I feel the same. I don't care what happened in there. Just give me another chance," he begs.

"I need to say goodbye to Cal."

He suddenly smacks his fist against the door, rage taking him over. "Don't you dare go back in there to him, open the fucking door!"

I ignore him and close the door. He bangs and kicks it yelling my name.

Cal looks worried. "Sorry," I whisper, and he moves the hair from my face.

"Thought it was too good to be true," he smiles kissing my nose. "Do you know how long I have fantasized about that exact moment?" he asks, and I smile shyly. "You deserve to be treated like a queen, don't let him treat you any less. Go before he explodes."

When I open the door, he is pacing the hall. He stops and then reaches for my arm, pulling me to him and wrapping his arms around me.

"You need to get a new personal trainer," he grumbles, kissing my head.

I smile and take his hand, "So can I tell people you're my boyfriend?" and he groans dramatically.

"I said so, didn't I?"

CHAPTER FIFTEEN

Aiden

I almost lost everything. Shit. The thought of her and him does something to my insides, something I haven't felt before, but I refuse to acknowledge it. It must have been the thought of losing the club.

I'm in the kitchen while she showers him off her. I dial Raff's number.

"Yeah?"

"Call the solicitor. Tell him to be here at nine tonight," I say, hanging up.

Bella

There is something more to this. There's no way he wants to be in a relationship, I can tell by the way he cringes every time I mention it. Then I hear him on the phone to someone about a solicitor. Nothing makes sense. He wants to cook me a meal tonight. Aiden, cook a meal? That just confuses me more and makes me suspicious.

He kisses me on the head, and I grip his shirt and try to deepen it, but he smiles and pulls back.

"I'm going to the shop to get us something nice for dinner."

"You would rather go to the shop than make up with me properly?" I pout, and he kisses my cheek.

"All in good time baby."

Now I am definitely suspicious because Aiden would rather die than shop, especially when I'm offering myself on a plate.

"I've got a few calls to make, stuff to sort out so I will be gone for a couple of hours," he says, and I nod as he leaves.

I head to the bedroom and start to go through the drawers. I need to know what he's up to and why a solicitor is involved. I check every compartment of his wardrobe and find nothing. The only other place I can think of is his office, but JP and Raff are often in there.

I call Aria.

"Oh my god you're alive, I was so worried."

"I need you to distract JP and Raff for a bit," I say hopefully.

"Why and how am I supposed to do that?"

"Aria please, it's urgent, offer them a threesome, anything that will keep them away from Aiden's office for half an hour."

"Okay, leave it to me," she says, and I hang up.

I search the kitchen while I wait, and she eventually texts me giving me the go ahead.

I take the elevator down to his office, my heart beating rapidly in my chest. I am praying he isn't there. I breathe a sigh of relief when I find the office empty.

I sit at his desk and have a brief look at the various letters and paperwork strewn across his desk. There's nothing that stands out. I open his drawers and find bills and random paperwork that means nothing to me. Maybe I'm being paranoid. I slouch back in his chair, huffing.

Something catches my eye under the desk, a middle drawer, set back so it's almost hidden. I pull it but of course, it's locked. Shit. I grab a paper clip and use the end to wiggle in the lock. I've seen it work in the films and to my utter delight it pings open. I laugh, I can't believe that actually worked.

In the drawer is a file, I set it on the desk and open it. I'm shocked to find that there's a couple of photos of me. One of me leaving work and one of me behind the counter at work. Someone has taken them from a distance. The one of me inside the shop has been taken through the window.

There's paper work with the heading Dobson Law & Co. I know that law company from town. I scan it and grip the desk in shock.

- Sexual intercourse must take place while Isabella is a virgin. It must take place between Aiden and Isabella.

- Proof must be given by GP examination unless other means of proof can be provided.
- Isabella must be fully consensual.
- Aiden must spend a minimum of eight weeks with Isabella and get to know her well.

This must be a joke. This doesn't happen in real life! There's paper after paper outlining all of Aiden's businesses. He has a 50% stake in everything and Jake, his brother, is the other stake holder. There's a hand-written letter amongst the paperwork, addressed to Aiden.

So here we are brother, I'm guessing if you're reading this, I must have croaked. I hope you gave me a proper send off, I know how tight you can be.

So, I can imagine you're reading this after Drake's been to see you. What I would do to see your face right now, I bet you are raging. Did you think I was going to make it easy for you? Just sign everything over? Come on bro, you know me better than that! What kind of brother would I be if I didn't challenge you one last time? Would you expect any less of me?

Bella is amazing, you will love her, and she deserves

to have a bit of happiness. My plan is that you will fall madly in love with her, but I know you will try and fight that. Bella is strong, she will make you see. I spent so long telling myself that I couldn't be with Harper that I wasted all the time I could have been happy. You are so consumed with the clubs and partying that you won't allow yourself to be completely happy. Laurie hurt you but you can love again!

I spent months trying to find the perfect girl for you and I figure once you have spent enough time trying to convince her to give up her virginity, she will have you hooked!

Don't fight it bro, I need you to be happy!

Good luck

Forever your annoying brother

Jake

I wipe the tears away. How can anyone think this is okay? I liked Jake. Me and Aria would swoon over him and his cheeky banter. Clearly Jakes plan hasn't worked because his brother really isn't in love with me. All of this is to take my virginity.

I feel sick and I can't catch my breath. This is what true heart break must feel like. I'm gripping my chest and trying to hold it together. I quickly shove everything back in to the drawer, wiggling the paper clip to lock it again.

I stagger back up to the apartment and head to my bedroom. I haven't sobbed since my mom died but as soon as I close the bedroom door I collapse onto the floor and shatter into a million pieces, sobbing so loud that I can't catch my breath.

How can anyone be so cruel? I really thought he liked me, all of the drama and the chasing he did, I thought that was because he genuinely liked me. Turns out that he didn't, not as a girlfriend and certainly not as a friend, because no friend would do this.

By the time Aiden arrives home I have gained control of myself again and I am sat on the sofa staring into space. My throat is hoarse from sobbing and crying. I sense him stop and look at me for a moment.

"Bella, are you okay?" he asks, "Have you been crying?"

I slowly meet his eyes, god I hate him. I want to dive

at him and punch his face until I make it hurt as much as my heart hurts right now.

He frowns at me. "Bella?"

"I'm fine, I watched The Notebook," I whisper. "It always breaks my heart."

He laughs and puts his bags of shopping on the kitchen table.

"What have I told you about watching romance crap? It isn't real, life doesn't work like that!"

"It's all lies," I blurt out and he freezes.

"What is?" he asks.

"Love, I don't think it exists in a world where everyone is so selfish and looking after their own interests."

He nods, relief flooding his face. "Finally, you see!"

Aiden

I cook duck breasts with vegetables. Not exactly Gordan Ramsey but its edible. I set the table up with candles and flowers. I've even pulled out on a bottle of champagne. Hopefully by the end of tonight I will have something to celebrate.

Bella isn't herself. She's quiet and withdrawn, like her mind is somewhere else. I've asked her to talk to me, but she just smiles and tells me it was the stupid film she watched, ruining her mood.

I pull out her chair and she sits.

"Looks lovely," she says quietly. "And champagne, what's the occasion?"

"Can't I spoil you?" I smile, pouring some into her glass. I've not even pulled the bottle away before she picks it up and drinks it down in one go. I frown, and she places her glass under the bottle neck for me to refill. "Careful Bells, this is expensive shit, you will be on your back," I joke.

"That's how you want me isn't it?" she says sarcastically, drinking down half of the new glass.

I'm worried, she is acting weird. I feel like she's looking at me differently. Gone are the smiles and playful kisses. She's not making sense. Something is off tonight.

She suddenly stands, and it takes me by surprise. I spill some champagne onto the table.

"I forgot the playlist, I did it for you while you were out," she says excitedly. "It's what couples do isn't it?" she adds, skipping off to her room.

I sit there quietly, wondering what the hell is going on. She returns with her iPod and connects it to the built-in speakers. Gnash "I Hate You, I Love You," fills the room and she sits back down smiling.

We eat in silence, occasionally she sings the lyrics *I hate you*. I'm wondering if she's singing those words to me. My concern deepens when Eminem's "Love the Way You Lie" comes on.

I fidget uncomfortably, if only she knew how these songs were so close to the truth, but she doesn't seem to be taking any notice apart from humming the odd part, a far-away look in her eyes.

"Not exactly love songs Bells!" I joke, and she grins.

"No but all songs I love. They have meaning!"

When Beyoncé "The Best Thing I Never Had" comes on, I stand to clear the plates. Her song choice makes me feel uncomfortable and I can't look her in the eye.

"Wow look at the time," she sighs. "Eight thirty already, any plans?"

I busy myself rinsing dishes and I feel her approach me. Her arms wrap around my waist and she presses kisses to my back.

"No plans," I say. "What did you have in mind?" I turn in her arms and kiss her on the top of the head.

"Maybe we could make up properly?" she suggests, and I grin. This couldn't work out much better, she's making this easier than I thought. Maybe the odd behavior is because she's nervous.

I lean down to kiss her gently, slowly brushing her lips with my tongue until she gives me entry. I walk her backwards towards the bedroom. I've left the latch off the front door and I leave the bedroom door open.

She lowers onto the bed, not breaking our kiss and I crawl over her until she's laying down. I try to slow down, keeping in mind what she said earlier about that bastard being gentle. Jesus why am I thinking about that now, and why do I care? Gentle isn't me. I fuck, I don't make love.

I stop, and she looks at me concerned. "Are you okay?" she asks, I see hope in her eyes and I'm not sure why that sends a dagger to my heart.

I've got to get my head in the game, I can't blow this. I give my head a shake as if that will clear all the crap I've got flying around in there.

"Yeah, sorry," I whisper, and I kiss her, this time hard and demanding. I move my kisses down her body, pulling her top down as I go. She's not responding right, and I glance up. There's a tear rolling down her cheek and I sit up.

"Bella what's going on? You've been acting weird all night. Am I pushing you too fast?"

She sits up, wiping the stray tear quickly.

"No, I'm just nervous, I want this, honest." She throws a leg over me and places herself in my lap, wrapping her arms around my neck and kissing me hard and desperately.

I have to just get this shit done. "It's okay, I've got you," I whisper.

She stands and removes her clothing. I take a moment to appreciate her golden, soft skin. Her curves are in all the right places. I'm going to miss having her body pressed against mine. The way she moans my name. I won't be forgetting her in a hurry. Her being here, in my apartment every night has been comforting.

She reaches for my shorts and I lift slightly so she can remove them. When she stands again, I grab her and throw her on to the bed. She squeals but I don't give her time to recover before I'm on top of her, kissing my way down her body. I run my tongue along her entrance and she bucks against me. Gently I push my finger inside and she groans, when I add another she cries out.

I circle her clit with my tongue and gently move my fingers back and forth, opening her up. She's so tight that I'm struggling to hold myself back from driving my cock straight into her.

She's gripping the bed sheets and panting. I can't take

anymore, I have to be inside her. I subtly check my watch, it's ten minutes until Drake is going to arrive.

"Are you on the pill," I ask moving back up her body, peppering light kisses as I go. She nods. "Are you sure about this?" She nods again. "I need words Bells."

"Yes, I'm sure," she says quietly, sounding anything but sure.

CHAPTER SIXTEEN

Bella

I open my legs wide to accommodate his huge body. I just need it over with. I might be giving him exactly what he wants but once this is over with, I will be free of this thing that's been over my head for far too long.

It's a deal that suits us both, maybe if he had told me from the start what was going on, I still would have done this. I fancy him, he's good at the whole foreplay thing and it's not like I was hanging on to my virginity for marriage or anything. The fact that he lied and pretended to like me is what's hurting me the most.

My heart wants him to stop, to confess to me about everything and tell me how he's realized that he can't go through with it, but I see the determination in his eyes, he doesn't care.

He places himself at my entrance and I hold my breath. I don't know what to expect and he gently kisses my nose.

"Breathe," he whispers. "Relax." As I try to force myself to relax, he pushes forward.

I cry out, the pain is intense, and tears run down my face. I'm not sure if I am crying because of the pain, the situation or because my heart cracks completely. He did it, he took it.

He stills and kisses my tears.

"Sorry, I know it's uncomfortable, it gets better I promise."

He smiles. I turn my head to the side and he buries his head in my neck, slowly moving back and forth.

I don't touch him, I don't respond to his kisses, but he doesn't seem to notice.

His movements pick up, sweat forms across his head and chest and his breathing is rapid and shaky.

"Jesus Bella, you feel amazing!" he groans, and I swallow the bile that's rising in my throat. "I need you on top," he whispers and with our bodies still connected, he rolls onto his back, moving me on top.

I notice the blood left on the white sheets where I had been laying. I wonder if he chose the white sheets on purpose.

I look down at him, I don't know what he wants me to

do. I feel fuller like this, but the pain has eased.

He grips my hips and I know it will leave bruises. He guides me, showing me how to move on top of him. I push against his chest, giving myself some leverage. He releases the grip on my hips and moves his hands to my breasts. The feel of him pinching at my nipples has me moving faster and I feel that warm feeling building up inside of me.

I lose control, I'm moaning, chasing that feeling. He grips my hips again and begins pounding up into me, it's all I need to send me spiraling over the edge.

I scream as tears fall down my face and he shouts out as he lets his orgasm rip through him.

"Fuckkkk!" he roars, squeezing my hips.

I fall onto his chest, my hands forming fists. I want to beat them against him. I hate myself for hoping that he wouldn't go through with it and I hate myself even more for letting myself orgasm.

"That was intense, So much better than I imagined it to be," he says, kissing the top of my head and running his fingers down my back lazily.

I stay still, pressed against him, hearing the footsteps approach the bedroom.

I turn slightly to look at the door, I look directly at Drake, Aiden's solicitor, who has the decency to look uncomfortable. JP appears behind him.

"Fuck man!" he shouts and turns away. "Cover her up!"

Aiden sits up, gripping me to him and wraps a sheet around my back. We are still connected even though he isn't hard anymore.

"Sign the fucking papers and go!" he shouts at Drake, who turns and leaves the room.

"Bella, I am so sorry, I forgot to lock the door…" I put my hand up and he stops talking. I stand, and he winces. I wrap the sheet around me and then head to my room without a word.

"Bells wait, I need to make sure you're okay."

I enter my room and close the door in his face, locking it.

He doesn't try to get in, he doesn't have a need to now. He's got what he wanted, he doesn't need to beg me anymore.

I sit on the edge of my bed, wrapped in his white sheet. I feel sore but it's nothing compared to the humiliation and hurt I feel.

I'm not sure how long I sit there staring at the floor, but I'm interrupted when there's a light tap on the door.

"Bella, let me in, I'm worried."

A bit late to start worrying now, I think, bitterly.

I ignore him and head to my shower, I need to wash him off me. I can smell his aftershave, it makes me feel sick.

I dress slowly in jeans and an oversized jumper. I thought I would feel more relieved than this, but I just feel so empty. I unlock my door, Aiden is sitting on the floor, leaning against the wall opposite my room, his head in his hands. Good, I hope he feels like shit.

He looks up, worry marring his perfect features.

"Bella are you okay?" he asks scrambling to his feet.

I walk around him and head in to his room, pulling my suitcase from under his bed. I go about filling it with my clothes, while he stands and watches, confusion on his face.

"When I first met Jake," I begin in a whisper, my voice hoarse from the crying and screaming. "I thought he was a twat. He came in every day at first and Aria was convinced he fancied me," I smile at the memory of Aria's teasing.

"What's Jake got to do with this?" asks Aiden and I look at him and give a small laugh.

"You can stop pretending now Aiden." Panic crosses his face. "I never, in a million years, thought Jake was so conniving and evil, because once I got to know him, I really liked him. I spent weeks laughing with him, listening to his tales of escapades that involved his brother, involved you! I had stories of my shitty life and all of the crappy bastards that thought they could get in my pants after one fucking drink!" I raise my voice towards the end. He flinches at my sudden rise in volume and presses his lips together in a hard line.

It must be hard for him to not be in control of this anymore, to not be able to take over the situation with his bossiness.

"And all along, he was plotting, checking to see if I was the one that could tame you, he was reeling me in and using me as bait to play a fucking childish prank on his dickhead brother! I liked him, I thought he was a good guy!"

I let out a sob and cover my mouth, trying to hold it in. He makes a grab at me, but I step back.

"Don't touch me!"

His hands fall to his sides. I've never seen him so quiet, without all the cocky banter he looks like a nice guy, but looks are deceiving.

I fasten my suitcase and place it on the floor.

"If you'd have just told me, if you'd have just said you needed my help, I'd have given it to you. It was never that important to me. I wanted to be friends with you, maybe more, but I would have been happy at friends."

I drag the suitcase through the apartment and towards the door.

"Where will you go?" he asks.

I shrug. "I would rather sleep in a shop door way than

be around you for another second!" I place my door key on the small table by the front door as I pass.

"I hope it was worth it Aiden, you may now be the sole owner of the clubs, women dropping at your feet, but when the lights go up, when the drunks go home, who's going to be looking out for you? This life isn't going to be amazing forever. You're going to wake up one day and realize you're an old man, still fucking a married woman that left your ass for better things, surrounded by fake ass friends that get their kicks from playing pranks on each other and you're gonna see all the good things that passed you by."

Aiden

I rest my head against the door that she has just closed in my face. I feel sick. She knew, all the weird behavior and dodgy songs make sense now, she knew.

I thought I'd feel happier. It's done, Drake signed the papers and I am now the full owner of two-night clubs and a bar. It's what I wanted, so why do I feel so shit? I'm never going to get that look out of my head, her disappointed, hurt face will haunt my nightmares.

I hope Jake is watching, I hope he can see the hurt he's caused. The hurt I've caused.

I let out a yell and punch the door, the wood splintering and cutting into my knuckles.

I head down to the club, it's quiet. JP is standing behind the main bar, his head resting face down on his arms. As I approach, he looks up. His eyes full of regret. The guys liked Bella, once they got to know her.

"Boss," he mutters. "Her face, she knew, didn't she?"

"Whisky, the bottle," I say, ignoring his question. He sighs and reaches for the bottle, slamming it down in front of me.

"She couldn't even look me in the eye when she just walked outta here. Like she was the one that did something wrong. It was us, we did that all because of some dumbass challenge!" I unscrew the bottle and take a gulp "Doesn't feel like you thought it would, does it?"

I slam the bottle down. "Fuck you!"

"I told Raff this was fucked up, I knew it would end like this!" he begins ranting and pacing. I pick up the bottle and head to my office, I can't deal with this shit right now.

I don't remember finishing the bottle but when I go to grab it, I miss, my vision blurs.
There's a bang and I make out a blurry image of Aria storming towards me, JP hot on her heels.

"You piece of shit!" she screams, and I feel the burn as her hand connects with my cheek. She gets in another before JP pulls her off me and holds her back. "Why would you do that, what did she ever do to you?" she yells.

I straighten up in my chair and she turns on JP.

"Did you know about this?" she asks. He looks away,

guilt written all over his face.

She pushes out of his hold, stumbling back.

"Aria hear me out," he tries.

"Oh my god, what is wrong with you all?" she gasps. "What gives you the right to do that to someone? She's in pieces, I don't even know where she is right now because she can't face anyone. She feels ashamed because of what you all did! How will she ever trust a man ever again?"

"There was no other way," I slur, and she spins to face me.

"There is always another way. You don't just destroy an innocent person like that, not for a club, not for anything. I thought you liked her, yet you chose a building over her," she snaps. "I hope it keeps you awake at night, knowing that you have crushed that girl!"

I have a feeling it will. I watch as she leaves, JP chasing her, begging her to listen to him.

CHAPTER SEVENTEEN

Bella

I open the front door to my home, the one I grew up in. The last time I was here, I met JP looking all big and scary. If I'd known then what I know now, I would have walked straight back out, refusing to even listen to any of it. Sometimes, ignorance is bliss.

"Dad," I call out and he pops his head around the kitchen door.

"Bella," he smiles, pulling me into a hug. He holds me at arm's length and looks at me.

"What's happened?" he asks, tears form in my eyes.

"It was all a lie Dad, he used me," I whimper.

His hands fall from my shoulders. "He went through with it?" he mutters, more to himself than me and then it hits me.

"You knew?" I whisper, and guilt floods his face. "Oh my god," I gasp, I grip my chest. "Please Dad, not you as well?"

"Bella, I thought this would play out and he would

make you happy, the way he sold it to me was that you wouldn't get hurt, he would make sure that you didn't get hurt," he explains, "You have this magic about you, I thought he would fall in love and get you away from this, from me and all the shit I bring to you," he says quickly, rushing to get his defense in.

I crouch to the floor, the pain is too much and any heart that I had left, crumbles. I can't catch my breath, I'm gulping air in between sobs. It actually hurts me to breathe right now. I close my eyes and concentrate; *in through the nose, out through the mouth, in, out, in, out.*

Dad reaches for me and I stumble back away from him, falling. I get up quickly, grabbing my suitcase.

"I just wanted my Dad, I just needed you!" I scream, and his eyes fill with tears. "You're not good enough, you're not a Dad, why couldn't I have a normal Dad? Mum would have hated you, she would have hated the person you became. I bet she's turning in her grave knowing that she left me here with you!"

He reels back, my words cutting him like a knife. I don't feel bad, he's hurt me too much. The one person that was supposed to be there for me and I can't think of one time when he was.

I leave him standing in the kitchen, clutching his chest, his silent tears spilling down his cheeks.

I walk around for a long time. My phone constantly vibrating in my pocket. When I stop I'm at Cal's door. I don't know why I'm here but I drag my suitcase up the steps to his door and ring the bell.

He opens the door, a look of confusion on his face.

"Hey Bella," he smiles. His smile fades when he takes in my swollen eyes and red, tear stained face. I must look a mess. He opens the door wider.

"Come on Bella, come in," he urges taking my case.

He sits me on the couch and goes to make me a coffee. When he returns, I fill him in on the story, from start to finish. I need to get it all off my chest and it helps me to make sense of it, as my words spill out. When I'm finished he lets out a long breath.

"Wow," he sighs. "That's some shit!"

He wraps his arms around me and I sob into his chest.

"Sorry for turning up here, you must think I'm such a

screw up. I just walked around and found myself here. I needed a friendly face and now you've turned into my therapist."

He smiles, rubbing a hand up and down my back. "Bella it's fine, I'm a great listener. Let me make you something to eat. Chill here for a while, until your head gets straight."

I must have fallen to sleep, I stir and stretch out. I'm still on the couch with a blanket over me.

"You stay the fuck away, if I see you near her, I will kill you myself!" growls Cal.

I sit up, he's speaking into my mobile and I instantly know it's Aiden. He notices I'm awake and disconnects the call. "Sorry, it just kept on ringing."

I nod and get up. "Thanks so much for looking after me Cal. I shouldn't have involved you. I just didn't know where to go. I knew if I went to Aria's he would have turned up," I explain.

He stands in front of me.

"I'm glad you came here, stay for as long as you need. I was looking to rent out my spare room anyway, you've saved me a job," he smiles.

"I can't stay here, I've already put on you enough," I refuse.

"Bella, please, stay. If you hate my annoying habits by the end of the month, I won't even charge you rent for that month and you can look elsewhere. What have you got to lose?"

The last time I made this decision I lost so much but I find myself nodding anyway. He smiles and picks my case up leading me to a room down the hall. It's decorated well, bright and airy. He turns to me.

"You can redecorate, we will talk about rent and stuff tomorrow when you have rested." He hands me my phone and gives me a warm hug. "Night Bella," he whispers and leaves me alone.

I spend the next few days feeling sorry for myself. I haven't left the apartment. I haven't been into work and apart from a couple of texts to let her know I'm okay, I haven't spoken to Aria. I feel ashamed of myself because even when I knew the truth, I went ahead and let him take advantage of me. I should have put a stop to it, ran as soon as I found all that stuff. I feel like it makes me as bad as him because I saw it as an opportunity to rid myself of the virginity curse. I'm not ready for all the questions that Aria will ask, especially because I know she will hate the answers.

I've had constant texts and calls from my Dad and Aiden. I haven't read or responded to any of them. What's the point? They have nothing to say that I want to hear. Cal took my phone and turned it off. Putting it away so that I didn't have to think about it.

Cal is around a lot, being a personal trainer gives him a lot of freedom. It's nice to have the company and he is so positive. He's turning out to be an amazing friend and I'm glad I turned up to his door because he hasn't judged me once.

He has me designing wedding cakes, he's set me up on a website and is convinced I can make a business selling my designs. I'm not so sure but it's keeping my mind busy and that's what I need.

Cal arrives home and I look up from my drawing pad.

"Hey," I smile removing my glasses.

He hands me a box. "I got you a present. Don't be mad, I just think you need this for your fresh start," he explains, handing me the box. It's a mobile phone with a sim card.

"Cal, you didn't have to do this, I would have sorted it."

"You can't do that when you won't leave the apartment," he says with a smile.

I get up and hug him, "Thank you so much, you're amazing."

He's right though, I do need to leave the apartment at some point. I like being here in this bubble. I don't have to think about Aria or Aiden or Dad. I know I'm hiding but I'm not ready to face the world yet.

Aiden

I stare at the bottom of the bottle, I drank that fast. I look around the club at all the bodies pressed together. I don't get the usual buzz, in fact it makes me feel empty. Laurie presses up against me, bringing me back to reality.

"Hey baby, you ready?" she asks, and I nod. She leads me to my apartment, ignoring my stumbling. She looks out of place here, in my apartment. It doesn't feel like a home with her in it, not like it did when Bella was here. I wanted to come home when she was here and now, she's shacked up with that fitness freak. The thought makes my blood boil.

Laurie lowers the straps on her dress and it pools at her feet. Her red lace underwear and heels should turn me on, but nothing brings me out of this mood I seem to find myself in morning, noon and night.

She bends herself over the counter and I'm reminded of Bella sitting there while I feasted on her. That thought gets my cock stirring and I approach Laurie. She grins like she's won. It's a good thing she doesn't see what's in my head.

I don't bother with foreplay, I just need to get my release, so I move her knickers to one side and enter her. She lets out a scream but doesn't complain. The last time she complained I kicked her out and fucked a girl in my office while she was outside screaming and yelling. I don't worry about pleasing her, I take what I need, all the time picturing Bella. Bella's tanned legs, Bella's Firm breasts, Bella's innocent eyes. I come on a roar.

Bella

It's been a month, a whole month since that terrible ordeal and I'm going back to work.

I've seen Aria once since it all happened. I think Cal warned her about asking questions, knowing how worried I was, so she didn't really ask much. We talked about everything but that.

She isn't seeing JP, she said she won't be with anyone that could allow something so cruel to happen. I told her she didn't need to do that on my behalf, they were good together when they weren't trying to kill each other.

When I enter the shop, she squeals and runs to me, wrapping me in a hug. "I have missed you so much."

I smile, "I've missed you too Ari."

We fall back into our routine of baking and serving customers and I feel like my life is getting back on track. Getting out the apartment was a good idea, doing normal boring things is what I need to move forward.

I can't think about Aiden, it hurts too much, but from what Aria tells me, he isn't coping very well. Drinking until JP has to carry him home. That pleases me. I'm glad what he did disturbs him enough that he has to drink to forget. He deserves that at the very least.

I show Aria my new website and the order I received for a wedding cake last night. I want us to do it together and she is excited to be involved.

"That brings me to a business proposition that I've been wanting to speak to you about," she says.

I stop and look at Aria who looks uncomfortable.

"Your Dad came to see me a couple of weeks ago," she says and I feel my walls go straight up. I busy myself with a cake mix but she stills my hand. "Bella, just listen. He gave me a check for you."

She pulls a crumpled piece of paper from her apron pocket. I open it. It's a check written to me, its signed by Aiden and I immediately hand it back to her.

"No!" I say simply and carry on.

"Your Dad insisted that Aiden write it out to you rather than him," explains Aria.

"That was good of him," I snap, sarcastically.

"I am on your side Bella, I told your Dad what I thought of him trust me, but I took the check because you deserve this. What he did was fucked up but why should you miss out?"

"I don't want anything from him, I want to forget it ever happened and get on with my life."

"With this money you can do that! The florist next door is up for sale Bella, with this money you can buy it."

"Why would I want a florists?" I ask with a laugh.

"Open it as an extension to this place, build up the wedding cake business, I can run the bakery and you can run the wedding side. Two separate businesses, but we can still work together and see each other every day." She smiles.

I shrug, "Sounds like you've already thought about all of this."

"You deserve this Bella. When will you get the opportunity to do this again?"

She's right, I do deserve this. I should take it, but something in me is struggling. It will feel like I've sold myself. Cal will know what to do.

Later, when I tell Cal, he doesn't hesitate.

"Take it Bella, you would be silly not to. Why should

you walk away with nothing? That scum bag should pay for what he did!"

"But isn't it a bit like selling myself, like he's paid me for my virginity?" I say, and he grabs my hands.

"He took it anyway, with or without the money. It won't change that situation, but at least something good could come out of it all. It's a big opportunity, too big to pass up on."

CHAPTER EIGHTEEN

Aiden

This is the first day in over a month that I've been sober. I miss her, I hate being in that apartment without her. She won't return my calls and for some time she wouldn't even see Aria or Jack. I did that to her, I made her so sad that she wouldn't even see her friends and it kills me.

The bank telephoned me first thing to tell me that Bella's check had been cashed. Originally the check was for Bella's dad, for his part in the lie. Of course, he never tried to sell her to anyone.

When he said he wanted it to go direct to Bella I tripled the amount and told the bank to inform me if she cashed it. That was weeks ago, and I assumed she had ripped it up when I didn't hear anything. This gives me hope, maybe she doesn't hate me as much as I thought.

I spend the day sorting out paper work. I've been leaving everything to JP and Raff while I was busy drowning my sorrows in whiskey and although they are more than capable of running the clubs, I feel like I should prove to them that hurting Bella wasn't for nothing. That I'm not letting the clubs go under.

They can't even look at me, I don't blame them, making Bella part of my life for those two months was a huge mistake. It hurt everyone, they all loved her and now she won't have anything to do with any of us.

Aria takes JP's calls, but she won't see him. It's killing him. I think he really does love the girl.

I'm left wondering yet again how this got so out of hand. What a mess.

Bella

I am so excited. I get the keys today for the new bakery. Work begins tomorrow to rip out the existing fittings to make way for the new ones. The new sign is going up later today. I am a shop owner.

Cal has taken the day off to help me. We want to start clearing it out to make way for the builders tomorrow.

I collect the keys and fling my arms around Cal. "I am so excited!"

He laughs, swinging me around. "I haven't seen you this happy in ages."

Aria joins us, and we step inside.

"No," says Cal, pulling me back. He lifts me into his arms, "You have to be carried over the threshold." He grins, and we laugh as he makes a dramatic entrance, with me in his arms.

A car slows down outside, and I get a glimpse of Aiden as it passes. My smile fades and my heart rate picks up. Trust him to turn up when I'm having a good day.

I decide not to tell the others. I won't let him ruin my

happy day. Why is he driving past my place of work? He got what he wanted and now he needs to leave me alone. I can only hope that seeing me in Cal's arms has given him the wrong idea.

The next few weeks are manic. I haven't seen Aiden since the day I got the keys, thankfully but then, I've been far too busy to notice anything that doesn't relate to weddings or baking.

The work on the shop will be finished today and tomorrow. We are having the grand opening. There's still a lot of work to be done and I have spent the last few days baking some of my creations to showcase at the opening.

I stop icing the cake I am currently working on and brace myself on the counter. I haven't felt well for a week or so now, dizzy spells and a constant tiredness. The business is taking it out of me already and I've not even opened up yet.

Aria watches me carefully, "You still not well?"

"No, I'm going to see the doctor if it doesn't go by the end of the week. I just want to get the opening out of the way. Cal thinks I'm working too hard and getting stressed by the shop." I sigh.

"And you say you had a period?" persists Aria

"Yes," I say. "I had my period as normal."

"Cal's right. It's probably just the stress," she shrugs.

The following day me, Aria and Cal spend the morning making sure everything is in place.

Beautifully decorated cakes fill the display cabinets and taste samples are carefully placed on table tops. Balloons with my logo across them bob up and down. There are iPads on the counter so that people can access the website to see more designs.

Cals put a clever app together where customers can design their own cake for me to make.

It's five minutes until opening and there's a few people gathering outside. Aria hands me a paper bag.

"I got this, just to make sure."

I peek inside, "Oh my god Aria!" I snap the bag closed like its burnt me.

"What is it?" asks Cal, and I blush.

"A pregnancy test," says Aria. "Just to make sure that this bug she's had all week isn't something else."

"I've told you it's not that!" I say, my tone high pitched and defensive.

"Then do the test," says Cal. "If you're so sure, it can't hurt, at least it will shut Ari up," he says. She swipes at him grinning.

I roll my eyes and huff, "Fine." I make my way to the loo and pee on the stick. I wrap it in tissue and stick it in my pocket. I have to wait two minutes for the results, but it's time to open the doors.

We stand outside, scissors in my hand ready to cut the huge red ribbon across the doorway.

"I now pronounce Bella's, open!" I say, cutting the ribbon. There're some cheers and clapping and I lead everyone into the shop.

I stand at the counter. I feel so happy, it's amazing how many brides have turned up to try my cakes. I have had lots of people register their interest today and I feel over whelmed. Cal was right, this is going to work.

"Did you check it?" asks Aria joining me behind the counter.

Cal leans across from the front. "Yeah Bells, did you

prove her wrong?" he grins. I open the tissue in my pocket, I'd completely forgotten. I peek inside. I quickly shove it back inside. Horror written across my face.

"What?" asks Aria, her eyes wide. I look up as the door opens, it's all too much.

Aiden stands in the doorway, his hands in his suit trouser pockets, looking casual and not one bit as broken as JP had led Aria to believe. The breath leaves my body.

"What does it say?" persists Aria trying to reach into my pocket, unaware that Aiden is stood in the doorway. I swat her hand away, not taking my eyes from him.

"Positive!"

"What?" Cal and Aria gasp in unison.

Aria notices that my eyes are still trained to the same spot and she follows my gaze to the doorway.

"What the hell are you doing here?" she demands.

It all happens so fast. There's movement and bustling. I hear Cal yelling and Aria is standing between them, but Aiden doesn't take his eyes from me. Cal is shoving and pushing, Aria is getting caught in the middle. Aiden doesn't react, his face stays calm, and his eyes are burning into me and in that moment, I feel like it's just me and him.

Me, Aiden, and our baby!

To Be Continued...

A quick note from the Author:

Wow, thank you so much for reading Aiden and Bella's story. I hope you enjoyed reading it as much as I enjoyed writing it.

You can follow me on social media to find out about new releases and offers. The links are at the bottom of this page.

I just want to say a quick thank you to some amazing people.

Paul, you are my rock and the reason I believe in myself. Without you marching out to buy me a laptop the minute I mentioned writing, I wouldn't have begun this journey! Xx

Owen for your constant support, for running my website and for doing all the tech stuff that I constantly battle with. Xx

Fay Della Rocca for encouraging me and believing in me. For reading my books and proofreading before they went live. I even managed to get your line in there! Told you I would. Xx

Tiffany Cotton for giving me my first review and boosting my confidence. A deal is a deal and I will gladly read out the hit list at your funeral. Also, for proofreading and being so eager to help! Xx

Finally, to everyone that reads this book, thank you.

It's hard to put a story that's been inside your head, down on paper and then let strangers read it, knowing that some will hate it.

But I hope that most will love it. Please leave a review on Amazon or Goodreads, it helps new authors enormously and boosts us enough to keep writing.

Facebook:
https://www.facebook.com/nicolajaneAuthor
Goodreads:
https://www.goodreads.com/author/show/18374765.Nicola_Jane
Website:
https://nicolajane582.wixsite.com/nicolajane

To submit a manuscript to be
considered, email us at
submissions@majorkeypublishing.com

Be sure to LIKE our Major Key

Publishing page on Facebook!

CPSIA information can be obtained
at www.ICGtesting.com
Printed in the USA
LVHW091803081020
668325LV00005B/1097